Galilee High

By Justin Strickland

Follow the movement on
Instagram - @hopeinkc
Twitter - @hopeinkc
Facebook - Justin Strickland

All Glory and Honor to God, Jesus Christ, and the Holy Spirit
who equipped me to write this novel.

To My Wife, Louise

Thank you for your patience and love during this process. I couldn't have written this book without you. You are the reason I push to be greater. I promise to always be greater tomorrow than yesterday while remembering you are here with me today.

To My Mom, Joycelyn

Thanks for instilling in me at an early age a love for books. You read to me and taught me that I could do anything. You were writing books before I was born and I guess the gene was passed down. This book is dedicated to you and for inspiring a life-long love for literacy.

To My First Teacher, Brenda

Thanks for giving me a head-start that I have yet to relinquish. You made reading and learning fun. Thanks for always being there for me when I need you and keeping me in check. It has been wonderful growing up as your first and favorite grandchild.

To My Sister, Jabrea

Thanks for showing me conflict and making me great at conflict resolution. You are a wonderful young woman with great things ahead of you.

To My City, Kansas City

Thank you for the many ups and downs you have shown me. I truly see the beauty in you and am glad I'm from this place. They don't make them like this nowhere else and that's the truth. Hopefully this book helps others see the beauty in you.

Chapter 1

Deuteronomy 6:5 "Love the Lord your God with all your soul and with all your might."

*P*rincipal Allen sat anxiously waiting to start the first Parent Teacher Association meeting of the 2015-2016 school year. He remembered when these used to run more smoothly, before basketball. When debate was the only thing parents were worried about taking too much time away from the biblical education offered at Galilee High School. Now, with basketball back for the first time in over a decade, he had forgotten all the problems that basketball had created causing the school's board to cancel it. Well that was the past and now he had to deal with parents, teachers, and coaches on the issues troubling those under his daily tutelage. He said a quick prayer and called the meeting to order, "Thank all of you for coming tonight. If you would find a seat and settle in we could get started."

Coach Slater walked in behind his wife, Mrs. Slater and daughter Jamaica, who would be attending Galilee

High for her freshman year. He loathed PTA meetings for the simple fact that everybody including his own wife ganged up on him. They all thought basketball was unnecessary and taking away from the Christian education at Galilee High. He nodded towards Principal Allen letting him know he was ready for the onslaught about to ensue. And sure enough it began...

Principal Allen started with, "I would like to open the floor to see if anybody has any glaring concerns this year. That way they could be fixed early and help our school give your children the best, Christ-led education possible."

"Well," started Mrs. Louise Best, "I think something has to be done with the amount of practice and games that basketball has because it is taking up way too much of my boy's time."

"The amount of practice time and games played by our basketball team is state mandated ma'am" responded Coach Slater.

"I personally love the discipline that Coach Slater has taught to my daughter and she has matured so much since the basketball program returned to Galilee." Mr. James Love decided to add.

"But what about our debate team that actually has won state championships and actually has sent our kids to college with full ride scholarships?!?!" Mrs. Best stood up to emphasize her point.

"Relax Mrs. Best, there's no need to get worked up so early in the meeting. We have plenty of things to discuss that I'm sure that you'll want to weigh in on." Principal Allen chuckled. He glanced at his notes that helped him keep these meetings on track. After the open session was the mission trip that they needed to decide on as a community. "Okay let's move forward in the meeting and discuss potential mission trips for this upcoming school year and costs."

"Where are we talking this year?" asked Mrs. Kierra Reece wary of the cost of sending her son to a far-away country.

"New Orleans, Cleveland, Detroit" Principal Allen replied matter-of-factly, "we are going to help better our own country this year."

"Forget our country! Why aren't we helping our own community?" Mr. Trayvon Gaines responded angrily. He always seemed to be angry, but at what nobody really knew.

"Mr. Gaines, we help our community on a consistent basis. The mission trip is a way for our students to extend the love of Christ to people outside our community." Principal Allen answered firmly.

"How much we talking?" Asked Mrs. Reece.

"Depends on how much we fundraise ma'am." Principal Allen responded.

"I have a couple of ideas Principal Allen, that the basketball team could do to help with that," Coach Slater stood up getting everyone's attention with his 6'6" frame. "We can host a Midnight Madness game and sell t-shirts to help raise money."

"My debate team could host an open forum on public events, where we sell concessions to help raise money." Countered Mrs. Slater never to be outdone by her husband.

"Great!" exclaimed Principal Allen, "Both of those are great ideas and we would use both of them to also support the efforts of your teams as well."

"Oh Principal Allen we wouldn't need those things to support our Debate team, we have sponsors who willingly donate financially to help our students." Responded Mrs. Slater gleefully. She turned and winked at Mrs. Best and smirked at her husband knowing basketball couldn't say the same.

"Well that is a relief on the budget this year, Mrs. Slater thanks for letting me know!" applauded Principal Allen.

"Mr. Principal Allen, I know that we have a tighter budget than usual this year due to state cuts so I'm willing to personally pay for some of the costs of this year's basketball season until I can garner similar support." Coach Slater stated winking at his appalled wife.

Jamaica Slater looked around after this announcement and remembered she was of course the only kid there. All of the other parents trusted their kids to stay at home alone for a few hours. She was reminded of how protective her parents were and after her parents just intentionally tried to one up each other. Their household was like nobody else's in the world! They competed in things like chores; they shot paper balls until people had to wash the dishes, take out the trash, do all the laundry, clean all the cars, and clean all the bathrooms! It was fun at times, but could also get real annoying, especially when her parents competed in public. They just couldn't understand how basketball and debate were equally important. Then again they weren't alone, only a few of the students at Galilee did both debate and played on the basketball team. Those students' parents usually leaned heavily one way or the other like Lionel Best's mom. Lionel was actually the only other kid Jamaica could think of that did both and there was no doubt that his mom definitely preferred debate over basketball. She, on the other hand was the best of both worlds. Her mom, the debate coach and her dad, the basketball coach. She was as balanced as can be!

"Wow! That's a blessing! See I've been praying and I knew that God would make a way for us to continue providing our young people with opportunities to participate in sports here at Galilee High." Principal Allen exclaimed.

"Amen." Several parents attending called out, Mrs. Reece being one of them.

Jamaica quickly sent a text to her 'mentor' on the team, Esther Love, telling her what had just transpired. Esther responded almost instantly saying that was great! Hopefully they'd get some new jerseys this year. Jamaica rolled her eyes and put her phone away. Everybody is always talking about all the money her family has from her dad playing in the NBA. If they only realized how much money her dad literally gave away they'd realize her household is much more normal than it may seem.

"Well one last piece of business before this meeting is adjourned," Principal Allen began, "I must remind everyone that this is the twentieth year anniversary for Galilee High! We will be hosting events bringing back old students and revisiting milestones achieved here by the grace of God over these last couple decades."

"Oooohhh!!!!!" Jamaica yelped, "Throwback jerseys!!!!" Picking up her phone again.

"Well I'm sure there are other things that have happened at this school other than sports Jamaica." Replied Mrs. Best

"There sure are! Principal Allen will we highlight things like the arts, academic achievements, and oh yeah will debate be a part of this anniversary?" added Mrs. Slater.

"Yes Mrs. Slater, Yes Mrs. Best, and I'll have to check with our financial situation Ms. Jamaica." Principal Allen responded accordingly to each statement and finished with a wink at Coach Slater on his last comment. "We will be looking back through Galilee history to find things to highlight. We will also be looking to put together a student committee to help us show our community the great people that God has blessed me personally to be in contact with. I truly hope this year will be the best year in Galilee history propelling us forward another twenty years."

Coach Slater nodded towards Principal Allen letting him know it was time to wrap up the meeting. Principal Allen nodded back before looking towards the parents.

"Well, now we will turn over the meeting to Coach Slater who will close the meeting with prayer. Thank you for your input and I look forward to seeing all of your children this upcoming school year as Galilee High offers the best Christ-led education that we can possibly give."

Principal Allen stated as he stepped down from the podium.

"Thank you Principal Allen and thank you parents for coming out tonight. Your support is one of the biggest reasons that Galilee High has continued its success over the past couple of decades." Coach Slater nodded towards all the parents seated. "Remember that there are refreshments in the back supplied from a few churches in the community that we would love for you all to take; I think there are some cookies, punch, chips, and some fruit over there. Feel free to take some home."

"Amen to that!" exclaimed Mrs. Reece.

"Bow your heads and close your eyes with me," Coach Slater began, "Our Father who art in Heaven, hallowed be thy name, thy kingdom come thy will be done, on Earth as it is in Heaven. Holy God we thank you for your time and your mercy. We are humbled by the ability to come to you in prayer and talk with you O Lord. We ask that here at Galilee we accomplish your will. That we do all things we can to further your plan and your purpose for our lives. We ask that we are able to put our own selfish desires behind us so that our flesh is removed out of the way. Help us follow you with our minds, hearts, and souls. You are the King of kings and Lord of lords in you is all power and truth and we thank you for your agape love for us. We ask that you protect this place and protect your people as we leave this place until we meet again. Bless the parents with wisdom to lead their children, the teachers with discernment on the best way to lead this school and the children with the ability to learn from all those around them. Bless the food and the people who provided it. Allow us to be blessed by our community as we are a blessing to it. Amen."

"Amen!" Responded all the parents, Jamaica, and Principal Allen.

Everybody got up and mingled at the refreshment table while the Slaters got up and left. Coach Slater was holding hands with Mrs. Slater and Jamaica typing away on her phone as they got in the car, heading to their humble abode.

Chapter Review

1. Where do you think that the high school should take their service trip? (New Orleans, Cleveland, or Detroit)

   _____

   _____

_____

_____.

2. Do you think that high school student-athletes spend too much time on their given sport?

_____

_____

_____

_____.

3. Should alumni that are successful give back to their alma maters? If they do should it be their high school or college?

_____

_____

_____

_____.

4. How important is parent involvement to the success of students in high school?

_____

_____

_____

_____.

5. Do you ever pray that God will humble you and show you how you can love him with everything?

How do YOU show God you love him with everything?

_____

_____

_____

_____.

Chapter 2

2 Corinthians 12:9 "But he said to me, "My grace is sufficient for you, for my power is made perfect in weakness." Therefore I will boast all the more gladly of my weaknesses, so that power of Christ may rest upon me."

Coach Slater walked back around to his side of the car, after making sure his wife was safely inside. As he got back into the car, he felt really pensive and began to think about his former life as a pro. He remembered when he first was drafted! His parents, wife (then girlfriend), and many other family and friends were in attendance. He never thought he'd see the day when he would play in the Association, but it was a lifelong dream that God allowed him to accomplish. Those first few years were rough especially because his wife insisted on staying in Kansas City, their hometown. This meant that he only got to see his wife and daughter sparingly during the eight month season. He still looks at those days as the toughest in his life, because of the rigors of professional basketball he needed his family, but they weren't there.

Dr. Slater looked at her husband knowing that he was thinking about his basketball career, or former career she should say. She knew because whenever he got real quiet, that's what he was thinking. She herself often thought about those days when she was a 'basketball wife.' Many people will never understand why she kept away from the NBA, why she didn't allow her daughter to live lavishly, but she had her reasons. She didn't want herself to get sucked into being lazy by sitting around the house all day while her husband played basketball. She didn't want her daughter to have to change schools if her husband was traded. She didn't want to be around all those other ball players who cheated on their wives, because she didn't want them to make her trust her husband less. She never wanted to be rich or famous like most of the girls she grew up with, she wanted to change her community, she wanted to empower black girls, and she wanted to do all this while teaching at her alma mater Galilee High School. She was forever grateful to her husband for allowing her to pursue her dream and not making her feel bad for not living the NBA lifestyle that he earned.

Jamaica looked up from her game on her phone and noticed that her parents were reminiscence quiet. She knew they were thinking about when she was little, when it was just her and mom, when mom wouldn't let them live with dad. She never understood why they couldn't go live with dad, why couldn't they go to all his basketball games. They usually watched on television, but she wasn't a normal fan, that was her daddy on the screen. She should be there in person to support him! All the times on video chat when they talked, daddy just talked about how much he missed them and loved them and wanted them to be with him. She cried every single time they hung up. She wanted nothing more in the whole world than to be with her father in the NBA. She always knew how to end the silence; she shyly asked, "Pops do you ever miss it?"

Coach was always surprised with how smart his daughter was. How did she know exactly what he was thinking? "Well," he started "I don't miss being away from my two favorite girls in the world." He was being one hundred percent honest, but he did miss competing on a nightly basis against the best basketball players in the world.

"You want to know what I miss baby girl?" Mrs. Slater began, "I miss the playoffs and how everything was so intense! Every time daddy's team needed a shot they passed him the ball and he seemed like he always made it!"

"Yeah, good times! You know what I can't think of any other way to have ended my career sweetie. So in that regard, I'm content" smirked Coach.

"Yeah daddy you're right! I bet all players want to end their careers by winning a championship and a NBA Finals MVP trophy. Michael Jordan almost got it right, but then he played for the Wizards...Daddy please never play for the Wizards!!" Jamaica pleaded.

"Hey the Wizards aren't that bad, so I can't promise that. I can promise to never play for the Philadelphia 76ers they may be the worse team in NBA history!" laughed Coach.

"Okay, deal!" grinned Jamaica.

Man his daughter truly was his pride and joy. He could see everything in her that was good in him and his wife. He literally wanted to give her the world! Growing up he could never understand how parents could spoil their kids so much that they became entitled brats. That was before he held Jamaica the first time over thirteen years ago, before her first words were da da, before she dunked the first time on her fisher-price goal, and way before she picked his number, 32, on her first rec team. A tear came to his eye as he thought of how wonderful his daughter was. Nearly as soon as the tear-jerking joy hit him, he also felt anger and grief directed towards his wife, who caused his family to be separated for much of Jamaica's young life. He remembers his parents telling him how wrong it was that his family didn't live with him while he played professionally. One night he remembered calling his best friend and telling him he was going to divorce his wife and get custody of his daughter. That was just anger though, he loved his wife with all his being and couldn't even imagine life without her. More than anything else he just wanted his family with him in Phoenix, not all the way across the country in Kansas City, KS.

Dr. Slater often thinks about those lonely nights when she would be home alone. Sometimes she'd get so scared that every time she heard a noise at night she'd call Coach and make him sit on the phone until she fell asleep. She brought her predicament on herself though and she knew Coach secretly thought she was selfish, but she felt God called her to live in Kansas City. God trumped Coach. Coach also tried to pursue God's calling for his life as well. Dr. Slater secretly thanked God daily for allowing their marriage to last through the pro lifestyle, through the long distance, and every other obstacle that the world could throw at her marriage. "What y'all want to do for dinner Slater family?" She asked the car.

"Pizza!" shouted Jamaica beating Coach to the punch.

"Well alright you have it, pizza it is! Babe can you order it online while we head home? Get a meatlovers and some wings." Coach Slater said turning to his wife.

"I guess that's okay since we haven't been eating out the house lately, but this isn't an everyday thing Jamaica." Mrs. Slater told the whole car.

Jamaica rolled her eyes because her mama is always trying to make sure she eats healthy. "Daddy is in shape and he can eat whatever he wants!" she pouted.

"Daddy buys his own food because he has a job" laughed Coach Slater.

"Daddy also was super healthy for the last twenty years, so he is catching up with the masses in greasy food consumption" Dr. Slater added.

"Hmph" huffed Jamaica.

"Whenever your child is speechless that's great parenting!" Coach Slater chuckled as he high-fived his wife.

Jamaica smiled to herself knowing she had broken the awkward silence past reflection always caused in her household. Then she texted Esther gloating about her getting to eat pizza because Esther's dad never let her eat anything like that!

Coach grinned because he absolutely loved his baby girl for always making his family better. Every time he finds himself resenting his wife for their past separations, he looks at his daughter and knows he can't possibly be mad at the woman who created such a beautiful thing. Man, she truly kept him going on his rough days.

As they pulled up to the house, the Slater family didn't seem like one who'd been through so much; on the contrary they seemed like the happiest family on the block as they laughed all the way to the door.

Chapter Review

1. Do you think that Mrs. Slater was wrong for not traveling with Coach Slater while he was a professional?

   _____
   _____
   _____
   _____.

2. How would you feel if you were in Jamaica's position? Would you be angry with your mom? Would you be angry with your dad?

   _____
   _____
   _____
   _____.

3. Are you able to bring people together like Jamaica did with her dad and mom? Or do you create more problems?

_____
_____
_____
_____.

4. Do you pray for God's purpose for your life? Are you living in that purpose or putting it off for the future when you're 'ready'?

_____
_____
_____
_____.

5. What do you think is more important God's purpose for your life or family ties? Could you do like the Slaters and walk in God's purpose regardless of how it makes you 'feel'?

_____
_____
_____
_____.

Chapter 3

Psalms 27:1 The Lord is my light and my salvation of whom shall I fear; the Lord is the strength of my life whom shall I be afraid

"Are you going to the black and gold game tonight?" asked Jabari.

"Of course!" responded Mr. Stills

"Well I just didn't know if they needed you down at the community center Pops" Jabari said.

"Doesn't matter what they need, son you come first" Mr. Stills told his son.

"Just me and you against the world, Pops" Jabari smiled.

Mr. Jacobi Stills would do anything for his son, especially since his wife passed away. He actually quit his job as a successful stock broker and became a community center director so that his son would have a free gym to practice in. Ever since he was little all Jabari wanted to do was play basketball; when his mom was alive it was her who supported him with all her time and after she passed away from cancer it was Mr. Stills who took on the role.

"Hey, Pops, we gotta roll! If we don't get started by 5, I'll be late for school!" Yelled Jabari up the stairs.

"You lucky I love you boy. These 5 am workouts are rough on ya old man" Mr. Stills replied walking down the steps.

"You should be used to it by now Pops, we been putting in this early work" Jabari said walking out the door.

"Yeah and every day I get older and older son!" Mr. Stills laughed as he locked the door and headed to the car.

Malcolm Abdul-Rahim was just waking up when Jabari sent him the text letting him know they were on their way. He'd started working out with the Stills since his pops died and Mr. Stills had become a father figure in his life. He enjoyed the early morning workouts because he and Jabari got to push each other and he knew he was getting better each day. He rolled over threw on his Galilee High sweats and hoodie and walked to the front room. Of course His mom was up making him eat breakfast before he left. She was always worried about him ever since his dad was killed by a stray bullet in a drive-by over a year ago. She just couldn't lose her only son. Their last year together had been rocky; with her finding Christ again after converting to Islam for her husband and then Malcolm himself struggling to find peace. She was extremely grateful for both Mr. Stills and Jabari who became like family after the death of Yusef, her husband.

"How's mama's baby boy this morning?" Mrs. Abdul-Rahim asked.

"I'm not a baby ma and I don't know if I have time to eat, they're on their way already" Malcolm responded.

"They can wait because you are going to eat. That doesn't make sense to go work out on an empty stomach son. You won't get the full benefit because you'll be thinking about how hungry you are. Then I'll look like the bad mom who doesn't feed her son breakfast. Now, you may not care about your reputation, but you can't be making me look bad!" Mrs. Abdul-Rahim said while she fixed his plate.

"Aight ma I'll eat until they get here" Malcolm laughed and rolled his eyes.

Malcolm sat down at the table to eat breakfast; which today was baked chicken, rice, and green peppers. His mom fixed her own plate and sat down with him to eat.

"Nu huh," Mrs. Abdul-Rahim reached to stop Malcolm from eating, "we have to say grace first boy you know that."

"Dad never said grace" Malcolm mumbled.

Mrs. Abdul-Rahim ignored him starting her prayer, "God thank you for waking us up this morning and providing us with clothes, a house, and food to eat. We ask that this food nourish our bodies and give us the energy to have a blessed day. Amen."

Malcolm waited then ate without saying amen. He devoured the food and finished right as he got Jabari's text saying they were outside.

"Ma they're here. I'm gone. See ya later!" Malcolm said as he grabbed his bags and left out the door.

"Bye. Love you!" Mrs. Abdul-Rahim called as her son quickly left out the door.

Across the city Mr. Love was waking his daughter up so that they could continue their routine of putting in early morning work.

"Dad not today, I'm exhausted!" Esther Love moaned,

as her dad shook her awake.

"You think Maya Moore didn't work out because she was tired, do you think Skylar Diggins takes days off because she doesn't want to wake up?" Mr. James Love replied as usual.

"Okay, okay, okay I'm up I'm up I'm up!!!" Esther called back, "And Papa they don't have to go to high school!"

"Once upon a time they did baby girl" laughed Mr. Love.

"Leave that girl alone!" called Mrs. Love, "it's too early James!"

"It's okay mom. He's right if I want to be the best I have to work the hardest" Esther told her mom as she headed out back to their full size court.

"Let's start with some stretching baby girl and work on some pull up jumpers today" Mr. Love said as Esther stepped outside.

"Alright Papa let's get it!" Esther smiled.

Then started one of their legendary tough workouts. Esther stretched for around twenty minutes before doing some conditioning. She ran suicides with each line finishing with a catch and shoot jumper. She then started at half court working on one dribble threes, two dribble threes, one dribble hesitation threes, two dribble crossover mid-range, three dribble step-back mid-range, one dribble crossover hesitation fade-away, and finally finished by swishing 25 free throws.

"Great work baby girl! I know there isn't a soul out there working as hard as you!" Mr. Love beamed.

"Whew! Just hope it pays off, Papa that's all I want is to be the best." Esther said as she headed back inside to shower and get ready for school.

She used to think there wasn't another girl in the state that could touch her skill level. That was before she met Jamaica Slater, her coach's daughter who started playing on her summer ball team last summer. Jamaica was four years younger than Esther, but almost immediately proved to all of her teammates that she could flat-out ball! That's when these early morning sessions with her dad started; she just couldn't bear the fact that there was another girl that could outball her, especially someone younger than her! Her mom didn't know that it was her passion and her determination that made her dad wake her up early in the morning every day. She sat down and told her dad that whatever it took she wanted to win State Player of the Year this year and bring home a State Championship to Galilee High. Ever since then, her dad has done everything in his power to help her achieve that dream. He put her in camps across the country, paid for private training sessions from the best trainers in Kansas City, and started this early morning ritual that he held her to without fail. He only hoped that he didn't push her too hard and he could maintain a good father-daughter relationship instead of just becoming coach-player.

The school bell rang and in walked Keith Reece the biggest teenager anybody at Galilee High had ever seen. He was a 6'9" 225 lbs. gentle giant that towered over everybody in the school. He was walking with the twins Carter and Martin Gaines the only other people in the school who could rival his height standing 6'7" and 6'6 ½" respectively. These three were almost always inseparable at school. Somehow they ended up in the same classes and had lockers by each other. Basically they just hung out all day. Their freshman year when they realized nobody was nearly as tall as them, they began going to the same classes regardless of their schedules and eventually the office got tired of marking them absent and made their schedules the same. They weren't bad kids either, did their school work, but definitely were the source of more than one class disruption.

"Y'all ready for tonight?" asked Keith

"Yeah, brah you ready? You the one 6'9" with no creativity!" laughed Carter.

"Man Carter you ain't got nothing on me anyways so don't feel bad K-easy y'all both gone lose the dunk contest" Martin laughed.

"Man I got some stuff y'all never seen!" Keith shouted.

"Man Martin dunk like he's a robot! He ain't gotta chance K-easy" Carter doubled over with laughter.

"Man y'all know I have the most bounce in the world!" said Lionel Best from behind them.

Lionel Best was a year younger than all the other boys, having skipped kindergarten. He was also the one of the smartest kids in school having scored a 34 on his ACT this past summer. Combine that with his insane jumping ability and he was one of the most versatile kids in the entire school.

"Man, y'all know I have the most bounce in the world!" laughed Carter mocking Lionel's high-pitched voice, "is your mom going to let you stay out that late? You know it starts at 8 pm isn't that after your bedtime?"

Keith began his famous laugh that filled the whole hallway with laughter. It made Martin laugh even harder, until he ended up on the floor in tears.

"Man you don't even sound like me!" yelled Lionel over the laughter.

"Leave baby face alone man. Y'all always on his case" intervened Malcolm.

"Yeah Keith you gotta redeem yourself from last year after getting hung, what like three times!" joined Jabari.

"Ohhhhh!!!!" shouted the twins pointing and laughing at Keith.

"Yeah brah we ain't forget about that! You giant embarrassment!" chuckled Lionel.

These were the members of the boy's team that were supposed to take Galilee High to the state tournament this year; Carter and Martin Gaines, Jabari Stills, Keith Reece, Lionell Best, and Malcolm Abdul-Rahim were supposed to bring the trophy back to commemorate twenty years servicing the community.

The group walked into homeroom with Coach Slater to begin the day.

"Hey coach" called the group as they took their seats in the back of the classroom.

"Hey fellas, y'all know the rules come to the front of the room" called Coach Slater before they could even sit down.

"Hey go ahead and open up your Bibles so we can start our day." Coach Slater said to the class.

"Hey I forgot my Bible coach so I'll just sit this one out" said Malcolm.

"No sir. I always keep an extra handy," Coach Slater said walking towards Malcolm, "here you go young sir."

"Can I lead the devotional today?" asked Jabari

"Certainly" responded Coach Slater.

"Well turn your Bibles to Romans 10:9. That's where we will study from today" Jabari said as he stood up in front of the class.

Malcolm turned open his Bible and just absent-mindedly flipped through the pages knowing he wasn't going to participate.

Keith put his head down, exhausted from working the closing shift last night at GameStop.

Carter and Martin turned to the right page and listened for the verse.

"Well the verse reads, 'If you confess with your mouth that Jesus is Lord and believe in your heart that God raised him from the dead you will be saved.' What does that scripture mean to you guys?" asked Jabari.

"Well it means that there is no other way to heaven" replied Carter.

"Yeah, you must believe in God and the life of Jesus exactly as the Bible tells it to truly be a Christian" added Martin.

"You must confess with your mouth. Don't forget that part" started Coach Slater, "we must vocally support Christ and tell others about his life. That's a part of being a Christian; arguably the biggest part is to tell others about Christ."

Malcolm was trying to figure out what all this meant. He was raised thinking about Muhammed not Jesus, but Muhammed didn't save his father or his family...maybe he'd give Jesus a try.

Chapter Review

1. How much do you think parent support helps kids become successful?

   _____

   _____

   _____

   ___.

2. Do you think parents having a confusing relationship with God or religion in general can affect the beliefs of their children?

   _____

   _____

   _____

   ____.

3. Do you think it takes waking up early and working harder to become successful or is that just something obsessed people do?

   _____

   _____

   _____

   _____.

4. Is there anybody that ever reminded you that you still had work to do and pushed you to get better like meeting Jamaica did for Esther?

   _____

   _____

_____

_____.

5. How do you think tragic events affect people's lives and their walk with God? Do they cause you to fear or become scared?

_____

_____

_____

_____.

Chapter 4

Psalms 27:3

"Though an army encamp against me, my heart shall not fear; though war arise against me, yet I will be confident."

*"H*ey girl!" shouted Jamaica as she saw Esther come out of class.

"What's up lil sis? You going to the Fright Night thing tonight?" Esther said walking towards Jamaica.

"Maybe. I'll have to ask my parents. It may be too late because of the Black and Gold events tonight" Jamaica responded.

"Oh yeah I can't wait until the three point contest! There's no way I can lose that! None of those boys have a chance" smiled Esther.

"Yeah, I just hope I can handle the pressure. I haven't ever done anything quite like this. I mean I can shoot, but everybody will be watching me!" squealed Jamaica.

"Well, I think you'll be fine. At practice you never miss shots. I hate when coach puts us on different teams and I have to chase you all around the court!" exclaimed Esther.

"Thanks Esther, I hope you're right. I mean I like practice, but it's just us you know? Y'all like family so I'm never nervous, but tonight there will be so many people I don't know. And you know people here don't even know my name they just call me coach's daughter." Jamaica complained

Esther laughed, "Girl you go out there and shoot like you know how and they'll know your name soon enough!"

"True, true" Jamaica laughed as they separated heading to their classes.

Jamaica headed to class where she felt so out of place. In her old school she was the B.W.O.C, or Big Woman On Campus. She could pretty much do what she wanted due to her great basketball ability. She wasn't unintelligent by any means, her mama wouldn't allow that, she had just become educationally lazy. Here at Galilee High though, they prided themselves on equal education responsibility regardless of athletic ability. So these first few months had been a readjustment for young Jamaica as she retooled her brain to active learning. It also didn't help that all of her teammates on varsity, her only friends, were older than her and thus in none of her classes. She struggled to relate with her peers, who went to different middle schools, before arriving at Galilee High and thus had their own group of friends come with them. Jamaica was the only one from her middle school that made it in, sometimes she wished she could go to school with the kids she grew up with. That was only hope because she knew her parents would never allow such a thing.

"Keith wake up" stated Mrs. Slater.

"I'm up, I'm up" Keith said, as he wiped slobber off his face.

"Okay well what will we be debating today?" asked Mrs. Slater.

"Ummm...school or no school?" stammered Keith.

The class burst out in laughter.

"Naw cuzzo we talking about if the federal government should regulate education or should it be on a state-by-state basis" said Lionell helping out his teammate.

"Oh okay thanks" Keith responded shyly.

"Now who would like to start off the debate?" Mrs. Slater asked the class, "Keith? Lionell? Either of you interested?"

"I'll go. This easy Mrs. S" laughed Lionell as he walked to the front of the class.

"Thanks Lionell. Any other takers?" asked Mrs. Slater.

"Yeah I can take Lionell, he easy meat." Carter said cracking his neck from side to side.

"Aww man! I thought I was going to get a challenge today. Guess I'll just think about a tough opponent" chuckled Lionell.

"Settle down boys" Mrs. Slater started, "We will be debating Presidential style. Remember it starts with a question and a response alternating who goes first with each question."

"Can I ask the questions Mrs. Slater?" asked Jamaica.

"Of course. Let's get started" said Mrs. Slater.

"Okay, first question: If we are all American why don't we all have the same education system?" questioned Jamaica.

"I'll be pro," started Lionell, "We should have the same education system. If you look at the other leading countries around the world education-wise they have nationalized education systems. China, Denmark, Finland all have systems set in place by the government that have been hugely successful."

"Well, Keith it is your turn" Jamaica said turning towards Keith.

"Aight, look that doesn't make sense. Finland and Denmark are the size of states so it makes sense they control their own educational system. Just like Texas and California should control their own education systems. It isn't like America's economy is the same across the country therefore the type of knowledge and work is specialized. As should our education system be set up to have students specialize in fields that they will eventually produce in." Keith said barely lifting his head off the makeshift podium.

"What about China? You addressed the size of both Finland and Denmark, but China is the second most populous state in the world." Lionell responded.

"Asians are naturally smart so that skews the statistics" Keith said cracking a smile. This comment caused the entire class to begin laughing hysterically.

"Settle down, settle down!" Mrs. Slater tried to get the students back on task.

"I mean all the kid geniuses are what? Asians. I rest my point young Lionell" Keith said winking at the class.

"Next question, next question" Jamaica said mimicking her mom trying to get the class back focused.

"I'm going first this time right?" Keith asked laying his head back on the podium.

"Yes, the question reads, should there be national teacher certifications?" Jamaica asked.

"Well, I'll be con again I guess...Ummm....No the way they certify teachers now is working just fine," Keith continued, " I think that because the states have different curriculum and teaching methods there are different requirements for each state. Um yeah."

"There should definitely be a national standard for teaching! What gives a kid in Arizona the right to get a better education than a kid in Kansas or Missouri? The separate educational standards are allowing teachers in different states to educate their students on a sliding scale. This is ridiculous to even think about. I mean we get upset about them getting a better education in Blue Valley or Shawnee Mission! What if we knew about what kind of education they get in California or Texas? Bet it'd start a riot!" Lionell screamed.

"Settle down young buck, you might wet ya diaper" Keith doubled over with laughter.

"Now Keith that isn't okay. Lionell is sixteen years old, he is far from being a baby" Mrs. Slater scolded Keith.

Lionell fumed sitting off to the side he hated that all the guys on the team made fun of his age. It wasn't his fault that he was too smart for Kindergarten. He told his mom that he wished she let him stay in the grade with all the kids his age. Her response was always the same,

'You are smarter than all the kids your age.' At moments like this he didn't feel smart though, even though he felt his arguments were better than Keith's. It seemed like everybody in the class thought Keith's speeches were funnier, more authentic, or something and he was barely trying. Keith got people to like him without trying just like most of the other guys on the team. While he had to constantly put in maximum effort for people to tolerate him. He couldn't understand why he just couldn't be himself. Well he didn't really know who exactly Lionell Best was, maybe that was part of the problem. Either way he needed to comeback at Keith or he'd never hear the end of letting Mrs. Slater fight his battles for him.

"Keith don't you have a beanstalk to climb up? Jolly green giant!" Lionell shot back.

"Well I guess we aren't mature enough to practice debate today. Those of you participating can work on your speeches for the tournament this weekend. Everybody else can study for the exam on Friday." Mrs. Slater told the class.

"Man I took this class thinking there weren't any test! You killing me Mrs. Slater!" Keith groaned.

"Sorry to disappoint you young Keith. Now get to work." Mrs. Slater responded.

"Uhhhh! Keith why you always playing??? Today was supposed to be my relax day! Now I have to do work!" Jamaica yelled at Keith as she went to her seat.

"Sorry princess" Keith said as he faked bowing in her direction. All he got from Jamaica was a roll of her eyes and laughter from the rest of the class.

This was a typical class period with Keith. Whenever he was awake he was witty, funny, and intelligent. The only problem was he was almost never awake thanks to the long hours he worked at Wal-Mart. He had even picked up another job at GameStop and going to work straight from school. Nobody really knew about his life though after school he pretty much kept to himself. The other kids didn't know that his dad was an alcoholic and his mom was addicted to prescription medicine. Even the twins, who most at Galilee would say were inseparable from Keith, didn't know that he paid his bills at his house and made sure his younger siblings, all three of them, ate and had clothes for school. This was the reason he'd never played organized basketball; he tried to play last year and almost made it to the first game, but his father went missing for a couple weeks. This episode forced him back home with the kids and off the team. This year he'd decided no matter what he'd play basketball with his 'friends' and use it to get a scholarship to escape his home.

"Hey yo Esther, hol' up!" Jabari called catching up to Esther after school.

"What you want?" Esther rolled her eyes in response.

"Dang! Is that how you talk to your future husband?" Jabari said pausing as he winked causing Esther to smile, "What you doing tonight after the Black and Gold events?"

"Wouldn't you like to know?" Esther said defiantly.

"Nope, just making sure you won't be where I am trying to cramp my style" Jabari laughed.

"You're not funny little dude" Esther said as she pushed him.

"Probably the funniest guy you know!" Jabari responded.

"Not! But I'm going to that Fright Night thing in the Bottoms, should be rocking" Esther told him.

"Oh aight I plan on being there too, wanna roll together?" Jabari said as smooth as possible.

"Maybe, I'm trying to get Jamaica to roll with me too. If she comes, her dad won't let you ride with me too. You know how he is." Esther said shaking her head.

"Yeah coach be tripping too hard, ain't nobody trying to get at little princess! I mean she aight, but she a baby." Jabari said walking out the school door.

"Oh so she aight?" Esther said rolling her neck, "Well Lionell ole baby self be acting like he like her, but he scared to talk to girls on posters let alone live ones."

Jabari doubled over in laughter, "Man, that's wrong. Y'all need to leave little Lionell alone because when he's the richest man on the planet he's going to remember all these little jokes y'all be cracking."

"Whatever I'll be richer than him anyways he ain't the only genius at Galilee!" Esther shouted walking to her car, "See ya tonight, get ya rest so when I shoot ya lights out you ain't got no excuses!"

"I'll let you know if I find these other geniuses and I could beat you shooting if I was in a coma so don't worry about winning anything tonight" Jabari laughed as he got on the bus.

Chapter Review

1. Do you ever get nervous when performing in front of people even though you know you practiced?

   _____
   _____
   _____
   _____.

2. Do you think it is easier to change schools and start fresh or go to a different school, but keep the same friends?

   _____
   _____
   _____
   _____.

3. Are you jealous of people that others think are cool, but don't seem to be trying very hard to fit in?

   _____
   _____
   _____
   _____.

4. Do you ever find yourself trying to be accepted by your peers? Why do you want to be accepted?

_____

_____

_____

_____.

5. Do you think outside events can hurt a student's performance in school? Should things going on at home come second to education?

_____

_____

_____

_____.

Chapter 5

Psalms 27:14

"Wait for the Lord; be strong, and let your heart take courage; wait for the Lord!

*F*riday nights were unlike any other night during the week, especially when basketball season started! Galilee High was hosting its annual 'Midnight Madness' again this year and the gym was filling up as usual. They tried to mimic a lot of the college programs and do it at midnight, but the kids would be too tired and they weren't able to convince enough adults to frequent the event so they changed it to 8:00 pm. This year they would be having a dunk contest and a three point contest. It was the official mark of the much anticipated basketball season and the school was buzzing with excitement.

"Yo...look at all these people!!!" shouted Jabari, "It has to be at least twenty fine honeys out there looking for a ball player!"

"So I guess that means they not looking for you huh?" Lionell came back with.

"That was too easy," laughed Keith, "Man it is a lot of people out there though, wonder why there are so many more than last year."

"It's because nobody had faith in us last year, but now they remember how good we were and how great we are expected to be. They bandwagoners that's what they are!" exclaimed Malcolm.

"Bandwagon or not, I see a bad dark skin shawty first row, and you know how Jabari loves the chocolate girls!!" Jabari said pointing towards the girl.

"Fall back little homie. That's my homegirl she came to see ya boy" winked Carter.

"Man she your homegirl or girl girl?" quizzed Jabari.

"She about to be my girl girl if she play her cards right" Carter responded.

"Sooooooo for now she's up for grabs! Like I said Jabari loves chocolate!!" Jabari doubled over laughing.

"Stop talking about yourself in third person" Malcolm rolled his eyes.

"When you get as good as Jabari, even you can't help but admire yourself" Jabari nodded towards Malcolm.

"Man this dude really got some problems huh?" questioned Martin, "Man, Jabari one day you are going to come back down to Earth."

"Oh definitely Martin," Jabari started, "but today ain't that day. So after I win the three point contest and the dunk contest, me and little chocolate drop going to turn up. Since Carter doesn't know how to close the deal!"

Everybody fell out laughing they all knew not to take Jabari seriously and also Carter would destroy Jabari if he caught him talking to that girl he brought.

"Esther why it seems like we are the only girls that care about basketball in this whole entire school?" Jamaica asked.

"Probably because we are! I overheard some of the other girls talking today and they were like 'I know Coach don't expect us to come tonight, we just play to get boys' attention not to win three point contest or try to dunk.' I was so shocked!" Esther said shaking her head.

"Yeah, sounds about right, well you win the three point contest, I'm going to bring home this dunk contest, and we can go home better than the boys" Jamaica said shaking Esther's hand.

"These boys won't know what hit them! I still can't believe you can dunk! I wish I could get up like that! Maybe one day I can be like you girl!" Esther exclaimed.

"Girl it is all my pops and his trainer friends. They know all kinds of training tricks and drills to help make you explosive. You should look into working out with me over the summer before you go off to school. I'm telling you they get you right!" Jamaica explained.

"Maybe, just maybe little homie" Esther started, "Well let's head to the boys' locker room for the pre-game prayer before we too late and coach try not to let us participate."

"Yeah let's roll; you ready to do this?" Jamaica asked.

"Of course" responded Esther.

Coach waited outside his office for the girls to come out. He couldn't believe that only his daughter and Esther had showed up. He had so much hope for the girl's team this year, but it seemed like only two of the players cared. At least it was the best two players he thought to himself they may just be talented enough to carry them all the way.

"Come on ladies, let's get this show on the road!" Coach Slater said as he saw the girls walking out of the locker room.

"Hey fellas, y'all ready to roll out and put on a show?" Coach Slater spoke, as he entered the boys' locker room.

"Yeah coach ain't that what they pay us for?" winked Keith.

"Well that's what they pay ME for, you on the other hand get paid with a free education" Coach Slater responded.

"Keith don't get him started! Let's just go, can I lead in prayer tonight?" Malcolm said.

"Um...yeah sure Malcolm" Coach Slater sputtered, looking around making sure he wasn't the only one surprised. Malcolm never prayed, most times he didn't even bow his head or close his eyes while others prayed.

"Heavenly Father," Malcolm started, "we come to you today, well tonight, to honor your name. We hope to glorify you with the game of basketball. Please allow our actions to be those you have ordained. We know through reading your Word that everything we do should be to glorify you and your kingdom. I ask that you bless all those standing in this locker room with your presence and protection this evening. Allow us to entertain those who have come to support us and stray away from injury. In Jesus name we pray, Amen."

"Amen!" everybody shouted.

"Hey man, where you learn how to pray?" asked Martin.

Malcolm smiled, "I've been reading my Bible more and it's something I picked up I guess."

"Well good for you!" Coach Slater patted him on the back, "Let's go put on a show!"

The two teams ran out eight players in all: Jabari, Malcolm, Carter, Martin, Keith, Lionell, Jamaica, and Esther. These were the players that held Galilee's basketball fortune in their hands for the upcoming season.

"First and foremost, I want to thank God for bringing all of us here," Coach Slater began addressing all the people in the gym, "thanks for coming out tonight to all of you. We certainly appreciate the amount of support being shown tonight and hope you enjoy the show! Now I will turn the program over to our lovely emcee for the evening, my wife, Dr. Dianne Slater!"

Everybody clapped as she walked up to the mic; she looked amazing in her dress. Coach even had to steal a glance at her as she sashayed by him.

"Everybody this is a blessing to be here and enjoy the talents of these young people tonight. There are two events this evening that we will have participants for. The first is a three point shootout with five spots and five balls at each spot with the last ball being the money ball giving a perfect score of thirty. The second event is a dunk contest where each contestant will have a chance to make two dunks in one minute, then each of our judges will give a total score out of one hundred. Speaking of judges we have some great people here this year! We have Principal Allen, our beloved administrator here at Galilee, Matthew Lee, a police officer here in our community, and special guest NBA veteran and Wyandotte county native Eric Walsh" finished Dr. Slater.

Everybody rose and applauded for the judges especially for Eric Walsh a legend in Kansas City for his athletic exploits.

"Now we will start with the three point contest, we will have five contestants: Esther Love, Jabari Stills, Carter Gaines, Lionel Best, and Malcolm Abdul-Rahim. May the best contestant win!" Dr. Slater said walking off the gym floor.

Esther set up on the baseline ready to start. She wanted to go first to put some pressure on the boys instead of the other way around. The buzzer sounded and she was off showing off her sweet left hand stroke. First shot up, good. Second shot up, good. Third shot, front rim. 'Don't be short she reminded herself'. Fourth shot, bottoms. Money ball, front rim and through the net on a shooter's bounce. Everybody roared as soon as the money ball went through and they cheered the rest of the time Esther shot the ball like the professional she wanted to be tallying twenty-three out of thirty points.

"Whew! That was a hot shooting round somebody might have to dip her wrist in some ice after that!" Dr. Slater started, "Now we will have Jabari Stills let's see if he can follow that up."

Jabari cracked his neck back and forth and swung his arms back and forth getting himself ready. The buzzer sounded and he began to dazzle hitting the first ten shots without seemingly touching the rim. Then he came to the money ball with twenty-one points and five seconds picking up the ball he blew a kiss at the rim for the point of theatrics and elevated. As the buzzer sounded all you heard in the gym was a *swish* as the crowd roared its approval.

"Well he looks like he needs some ice too, for his wrist and his lips!" Dr. Slater laughed, "Next up Carter Gaines."

Carter winked at Martin and proceeded to shoot the ball left-handed all the way around the horn. The only problem was he was a right-handed player. As the buzzer sounded and he made the last money ball giving him a total of five points he began beating his chest. He pointed at Martin and made a symbol for money. Martin just laughed as Carter headed back towards him.

"Well that was interesting...moving on to the next contestant Lionell Best!"

Lionel lined up with his palms sweating, stomach lurching nervous as ever. He knew he could shoot, but everybody was watching him do it. This was so different than practice or even games where there's always other players out there with him. He needed to make the first one he knew if he made the first one he'd be fine. The buzzer sounded he picked up the ball and shot...in and out. 'Oh no that's supposed to go in!' He labored from that point on with almost no confidence making some and missing more he finished with a decent score of twelve points. He was obviously distraught with his performance as he slumped off the court.

"It's okay sweetie you did good, didn't he crowd?" Dr. Slater elicited some claps for Lionel. "Now our last contestant of the night Malcolm Abdul-Rahim!"

Malcolm stepped up calm and collected he had told his mom he was going to win the contest tonight for his dad. He tapped his shoes where he had written his dad's initials on them and looked toward the ceiling pointing towards heaven. The buzzer sounded and he went into a zone unlike any he had ever been in. He didn't touch the rim until the money ball on the third rack which rolled around the rim and went in. On the last rack everybody in the building was standing counting each make. 'TWENTY-FIVE, TWENTY-SIX, TWENTY-SEVEN, TWENTY-EIGHT, THIRTY!!!!'

After the last shot went in he instantly broke down, weeping as his mom ran onto the floor hugging him.

Dr. Slater wiped her eyes, "Malcolm told me before the contest that he was shooting for his father, whom passed away this past summer. As you can see, that was an emotional performance that I know for a fact his father would be proud of don't you think?"

The crowd stood up giving Malcolm a standing ovation for his winning performance.

"Thank you, thank you" Malcolm said through tears, "I am truly humbled by your support of me and my teammates tonight. I appreciate all of you sharing that moment with me, I will never forget that for the rest of my life." Malcolm grabbed his plaque and walked back to the bench with his head held high.

"Great job fam! That's how you shoot the basketball bro!" Jabari dapped Malcolm up as he got back to the bench.

"Moving on! We will have our dunk contest featuring: Jamaica Slater, Martin Gaines, Keith Reece, and Lionel Best. As my husband loves to say, 'Let's Hoop!'" Dr. Slater said walking towards the sideline.

Jamaica pumped up the crowd by raising both her arms, getting them to join in on her dunks. She grabbed the ball, took two bounces, and attacked the basket taking two steps and turning 180° doing a reverse dunk cleanly. The crowd went crazy!!! Jamaica smiled, she had been working all summer for this moment. She turned and winked at her dad, who just winked back with the biggest, proudest smile on his face. For her second dunk she had Esther go into the crowd and throw her an alley-oop. The ball bounced perfectly, just like they practiced and Jamaica caught it in her right hand, throwing down another perfect dunk. The crowd erupted with several fans running on the floor and all the judges standing up holding up three hundred points for a perfect score.

"Well, bet you've never seen something like that!" Dr. Slater said proudly, "Jamaica gets a perfect score giving Martin Gaines a tough act to follow."

Martin took the floor knowing what dunks he was going to do and as the clock started he walked to the opposite free throw line. He started sprinting and jumped from the free throw line where he spread his legs mimicking Jordan and threw down a nice dunk. The crowd clapped, but didn't respond with nearly the same enthusiasm as when Jamaica dunked. He then threw the ball up from the baseline catching it with his right hand switching to his left hand as he went under the rim dunking it hard on the opposite side. This dunk got much more fanfare and Martin winked at Carter as he went to sit down. The judges stood with Principal Allen giving a 75, Matthew Lee gave a 74, and Eric Walsh gave an 81 for Martin's exploits above the rim.

"Those are pretty good scores right there! 240 points isn't too shabby, good job Martin! Let's see what the big fella Keith Reece can follow up with" Dr. Slater spoke in the microphone.

Keith Reece got up just wanting to beat Martin he didn't need to get a perfect just enough to win their bet. For his first dunk he started on the left side of the court, just outside the three point line. The clock started, he took two steps then he jumped in the air and turned in a complete 360 throwing down the ball with two hands as he came back around. The crowd again was excited and jumped out of their seats. Keith smiled and immediately went into his next dunk to keep the momentum. Starting at the free throw line, he threw the ball up backwards before doing a back flip, turning, and catching the ball with his left hand dunking it through. The judges jumped out of their seats giving Keith a close to perfect score as he ended up with 283 points edging out Martin. Keith had won the bet with the twins, Carter and Martin, winning something more important to him than a plaque...money. "I told you not to bet on Martin beating me," Keith told Carter walking back to the sideline, "Now you gotta both pay up!"

"Who knew someone with that much size could be so explosive?! Thankfully he plays for us or he'd be a problem on the court! Let's give it up for our last contestant Lionell Best!" Dr. Slater finished excitedly.

Lionell wasn't kidding when he said he was the highest jumper in the city, he had a forty-six inch vertical jump! He had been practicing for this dunk contest over and over in secret because he wanted to win so badly. Last year he had missed a couple dunks and ruined his chances for victory, but this year he knew his practice would pay off. The only thing he was upset about was Jamaica dunking; nobody had any clue she could bounce like that! He took the floor on the right wing and faked like he was about to take to the rim before telling the crowd to wait one second while he put up the number one with his fingers. He then took off his Galilee jersey revealing a throwback Toronto Raptors Vince Carter jersey underneath. He immediately exploded like a rocket to the rim, jumping in a full circle while bringing the ball from his chin back to his chin in a full windmill motion before dunking the ball so hard it almost bounced off the floor and back through the net! The crowd went nuts; people were screaming, people were running around the bleachers, a couple people pretended to pass out, his dunk caused sheer pandemonium. He then brought out a chair asking his mom, his best practice partner, to sit in it. He started in the middle of the floor about at half-court. She bounced the ball in front of her and her son leapt over her as graceful as anybody could imagine catching the ball low and going between his legs dunking it with authority. It was too much authority though as the ball hit the back of the rim, the crowd let out a sigh of disappointment. Lionell immediately smiled and asked the crowd for one more chance. This time he didn't disappoint, seemingly jumping higher and dunking harder than he did the first time clearing his mom with room to spare. The crowd reacted accordingly, coming to its feet instantly!

"Whoa!!!" Dr. Slater shouted running on the floor, "now that was a show ladies and gentlemen! Let's see what the judges have to say: Principal Allen with 100, Matthew Lee with another perfect score, and Eric Walsh with a 99. Oh! So close to a perfect score ladies and gentlemen!!! Well that makes Jamaica Slater our winner for the dunk contest. Thanks for coming out! We hope to see you at our games this year and don't forget to grab a schedule on your way out. There are three schedules on the table girls' basketball, boys' basketball, and debate out in the foyer as you leave we appreciate your support for all of our extracurricular activities."

"Thanks to all of you for coming" Principle said as Dr. Slater handed him the mic, "Let me pray us out please. Heavenly Father, we thank you for today. We thank you for bringing us here and blessing us with the opportunity to enjoy the talents of these young people. We ask that all those in attendance are blessed with your love and your spirit as we leave this place until we meet again. Amen. Goodnight everybody!"

Chapter Review

1. Are you patient waiting on God to answer your prayers?

   _____

   _____

   _____.

2. Do you think that community support makes a team better or a good team makes the community support?

   _____

   _____

   _____.

3. Do girls take sports as seriously as boys? Are they supported as much?

   _____

   _____

   _____.

4. Should parents be strict on their kids on who they ride with and hang out with even if they're in high school?

   _____

   _____

   _____.

5. How do you feel about extracurricular activities in high school? Are they necessary? Do sports outshine everything else in public support? Is that fair?

_____

_____

_____.

Chapter 6

Exodus 20:12

"Honor your father and mother, that your days may be long in the land that the Lord your God is giving you."

"**W**ake up Jamaica! You are not going to make us late! I'm the coach! I can't be late!" Mrs. Slater shouted up the stairs. "Girl, nobody told you to go to that darn Fright Night last night! You knew our first debate tournament was today! Josiah, you better get your daughter before you become childless today! She is making me late!"

Coach Slater laughed as he headed up the stairs to wake up his baby girl. He already knew this morning was going to be an issue, with Galilee High having their first debate tournament. Debate isn't like basketball, they have to get up early on Saturday morning, usually around six am, to get on the bus and travel to a tournament that lasts all day.

"Baby girl, you have to wake up before you make my wife have a heart attack. You know how nervous she gets before these things" Coach Slater said.

"Uhhh Papa! I'm still exhausted from last night" Jamaica groaned.

"I know sweetie, but you know you have to keep your word. You signed up for the debate team and now it is time to debate. Your word is bond you know that," Coach Slater reminded his daughter.

Jamaica rolled her eyes, "Here I come Papa. Tell mama bear to relax I'll be ready quickly."

Coach Slater chuckled, "I'll let her know to take a chill pill and you hurry up so I don't end up dying in the crossfire."

Mrs. Slater paced back and forth waiting on her daughter. She was always nervous before the first tournament and this year she was especially nervous. They were coming off of their first ever state championship, so big things were expected from this team. She hoped Lionell Best could step in and assume the role of captain this year, he was intelligent and fiery, perfect for the role. His only problem was he tended to forget to use his passion during debates and ended up sounding like a robot stating facts. She hoped that her daughter could bring a different perspective to the team, being the only girl on Varsity this year. Her secret weapon was Carter Gaines, he had asked to be on the team after tryouts and she obliged. She allowed him to practice on his own since he had a job and basketball practice. She heard him practice once a week and he was amazing. She just hoped that he didn't freeze up on the big stage.

"Okay ma, I'm ready, let's go!" Jamaica yelled coming down the stairs.

"Good I'm only 300 years old now. Thought I'd reach a thousand before I saw your face" Mrs. Slater fumed.

"Well, ma I must say you are a young looking 300 year old. You don't look a day over 190!" Jamaica laughed.

"Watch it little girl, my wife don't look a day over 70!" Coach Slater couldn't resist getting in on the joke.

"Hardy har har. Y'all are just so funny. You should take this show on the road" Mrs. Slater sarcastically said.

        The Slaters left the house and headed towards the school. Once there Mrs. Slater got her schedule and credentials out of her office and talked with the bus driver as the kids arrived. There were 5 kids on the team: Jamaica Slater, Carter Gaines, Lionell Best, Howard Riley, and Gerell Davis. She knew Howard and Gerell were completely dedicated to the team; they both looked at debate as a way to get into college and potentially as a career. She felt bad because although they were hard workers, she honestly didn't think they gave the team the best chance to win. The two best speakers on the team were Carter Gaines and Lionell Best. Lionell spoke with eloquence and could articulate exactly what the research said. Carter had a knack for making research real, he could take numbers and data and force the judges to see real people. The only thing about Carter was he wasn't battle tested; he had never debated in a tournament or even at debate practice. All his work she'd seen from him was during lunch, when it was just her and him in her classroom. She hoped he didn't freeze up when the opportunity arose for him.

"Good morning all," Mrs. Slater said as she got on the van, "let's go get this first win of the season out of the way!"

"Yeah," the kids half-heartedly responded, "let's do this."

"Whoa, whoa, whoa! Where's the passion?!" Mrs. Slater exclaimed.

"Passion doesn't wake up until at least 9 in the morning Dr. Slater. When it arrives I'll let you know" Carter sleepily replied.

"Okay understandable, understandable. Well let's at least be prepared. If we're going to be boring we will be the most informative, boring debate team ever" Mrs. Slater laughed. "First things first, what is the resolution this season?"

"Well," Gerell Davis began, "this season's resolution is 'That the federal government should adopt a nationwide policy to decrease overcrowding in prisons and jails in the United States.'"

"Affirmative argument?" Mrs. Slater asked.

"I'll take this one," Howard Riley started, "The fact that over 16 states in this country now have more people jailed than in colleges, according to MetricMaps is astonishing. It causes us to reevaluate the priorities this country has. Also according to an article by theGrio.com crime has dropped steadily over the past few decades with prison population and spending constantly increasing."

"Okay, we can tackle the priority thing Howard. Because since they are spending much more on prisons they can't spend this money on education. Any numbers on that discretion?" Carter replied.

"Yes. In Alabama one of the states with more prisoners than college students, the rate of spending for prisons increased by 45% over a four year period while the spending on education only increased 7.5%." Howard continued.

"That's good. Anything else?" Carter asked.

"Yeah the United States has more people imprisoned than any other place in the world, yet has fallen behind in education to number 14 in the world, according to learningcurve.com" Howard finished.

"Okay thanks Howard. I'm ready, time to nap." Carter said putting his headphones on.

"Well, now that we have the affirmative, here is the negative argument," Gerell Davis began, "The federal government doesn't have the authority to affect every state's penal system. In that same article by theGrio.com it states that places like Louisiana have different conviction laws than say a place like Kansas. These irregularities could cause the federal government to enact laws and force state spending in places where both are unnecessary. The South needs to regulate its prison population, not the whole country. In article eleven of the sixteen states are Southern states. This is a state issue not a national one."

"Okay, what else you have? I can see that angle, but we need something a little bit stronger. They may argue that the national government make it a state priority. Then what else will we have?" Lionel interjected.

"Hmm...well you could argue that the people overpopulating the prison system are prisoners. They have broken laws and deserve to be in prison. It isn't a federal government issue, but a parental and community issue" Gerell answered.

"That's a great argument. All types of places I could take that one! Thanks man! We will be fine today. Mrs. Slater can we nap now? It is 6 in the morning after all" Lionell said lowering his cap over his eyes.

"Okay, hope y'all ready" Mrs. Slater said.

They pulled up to the school after two hours on a bus. Mrs. Slater always tried to schedule the first debate tournament far away from the school in order to hide their arguments from their closer competition. This year their first tournament was in Wichita, KS well outside their immediate competitors boundaries. She was pretty confident the competition level wouldn't be too tough and they would be able to make the finals without much trouble. She wanted to make sure they were ready for the steeper competition. She had too many new faces on the team to throw them in the immediate fire.

Jamaica just looked around in awe at the amount of kids at the tournament. This is so much more intense than basketball. All these people here are participants, not just fans they are actually trying to beat you!

"Mom!" Jamaica squealed, "Why didn't you say all these people were going to be here?"

"Huh? Jamaica, you tripping this tournament is small! There aren't nearly as many people here that will be at our later tournaments this is just a warm-up for us" Howard laughed.

"Yes, sweetie Howard is right. This is something light" Mrs. Slater added.

"Well let's get this party started y'all! Who we beating first?" Carter asked the team.

"Let's check the schedule and see what room we are in" Mrs. Slater said while she directed the kids toward the board.

The beginning of the tournament went as Mrs. Slater expected. Carter was amazing in personifying the statistics, while Lionell was apt at battling everybody's responses to their arguments. The team had been lucky up to this point and had gotten the affirmative, or pro, side of each argument, which is better because you are allowed to define the resolution from your own perspective. They moved on to the finals pretty easily as the judges loved the mix of Lionell's seriousness and Carter's personality.

"Okay everybody we've done great thus far. Let's bring this championship home! This will be a little tougher. I've watched the team we are going against and they are the best team we have faced yet" Mrs. Slater told her team.

"I've got bad news. We lost the coin toss, we have neg" Gerell somberly said to his teammates.

"What the heck does neg mean?" Carter asked.

"It means we are arguing the negative. The other team will be able to set the resolution. We haven't done that all day! I hate it when they wait until the finals to make you argue the opposite" Howard answered.

"That's tough. I saw them and they've been setting their resolution for secret and military prisons" Mrs. Slater shook her head.

"Huh? Coach we don't have anything like that in our notes or statistics. What will we do?" Lionell asked.

"We have forty-five minutes, so we will get work on getting some statistics for the negative side. Let's do what state champions do...adapt and win a trophy" Mrs. Slater spurred on her team.

"Welcome all to the finals today in the third annual Fall Showdown here in Wichita showing off high school debaters from all across the state. This year we have the honor of having the defending Kansas State debate champions, Galilee High, battling for the trophy against our hometown debaters, Wichita Southwest" the announcer started.

"I'm so nervous" Jamiaca whispered to Lionell.

"Why? You're not even debating? Chill shawty we will be aight" Lionell reassured her.

"The first team you will hear this afternoon will be Wichita Southwest as they argue the affirmative in this finals" the announcer finished.

"Thank you sir. Resolve, that the federal government should adopt a nationwide policy to decrease overcrowding in prisons and jails in the United States." The student on the Wichita team started, "The federal government must come up with a plan to limit the amount of secret and military prisons that exist under the control of the United States. There are countless international laws prohibiting such activity in places like Guantanamo Bay. The International Covenant on Civil and Political Rights contains an article, article 10, which says that any person deprived of their personal liberties deserves to be treated with dignity and respect. These prisons operate outside of the public eye with little to no accountability on the treatment of the prisoners held there. It is completely un-American to host prisoners without hope of a trial, without telling their families where they are, without even admitting what crime the government is charging them with. The plan of action is simple, we must close these secret facilities down. We must open new ones that are accountable not only to the American government, but the American public. Most Americans don't understand the horrors of these places until something leaks on the internet, but these atrocities go on daily and need to be stopped. Thank you" the student finished to applause by the crowd after his spirited constructive speech.

"Well now we will turn the floor over to Galilee High" the announcer said looking towards the Lions bench.

"Thank you judges for your time. There are multiple problems with this resolution. I'll start with the fact that these people are criminals that deserve to be jailed. Also you brought up Guantanamo Bay which is a place that prisoners are made up of a population majority of foreigners. These people aren't United States citizens, so why would they deserve to be treated as such? They have committed crimes that are completely destructive and planned to damage the US people. Also the secret prisons are nearly impossible to shut down. The amount of red tape and governmental secrets that bury the location of these places are extraordinary. These locations only exist according to conspiracy theorist, but there is little to no concrete evidence that suggests these places are real. How can you shut down something that nobody knows exists? I'm sorry to tell you, but the resolution you have stated and plan that you want to enact seems both farfetched and imaginary. Thank you for your time" Carter finished his passionate speech.

"Hand me the trophy please! Can I carry it on the bus? I want to take a picture on Instagram with it. I think it accents my dress" Jamaica said as they boarded the bus.

"You didn't do nothing to deserve this trophy Ms. Reserve!" Carter scoffed.

"Don't be rude man! Here shawty go ahead and take it" Lionell said taking the trophy from Carter.

"Be careful y'all just don't break it, so we can have something to put in our trophy case. I'm proud of you guys. That was a great tournament! Way to adapt and win. This is a great start to our state championship" Mrs. Slater told the team.

"Let's get home y'all. I'm exhausted this takes way more energy than basketball! I mean we been up since five this morning and we won't get back to school until nine at the earliest tonight" Carter laughed.

"Yeah I'm sleeping next to the trophy like MJ! Somebody take a pic and send it to me!" Jamaica said.

"Got you. Good job Howard and Gerell! We definitely would have been dead without your research in the finals round. Y'all the real MVPs!" Lionell spoke up as the bus pulled off.

"No problem, talk when we get home. I'm going to sleep" Gerell grouchily replied.

"Yeah everybody rest. Good job y'all!" Mrs. Slater said.

Chapter Review

1. Do you think that the prisons in the United States are overcrowded? If so, what should be done about it?

   _____

   _____

   _____

   _____.

2. Do you think that it's fair that Howard and Gerell do a lot of research, but never get to debate?

   _____

   _____

   _____

   _____.

3. Do you think it would be weird having your parent as a coach?

   _____

   _____

   _____

   _____.

4. Do you think it is fair that Mrs. Slater made an exception for Carter on missing practices, but still being able to debate?

_____

_____

_____

_____.

5. Do you honor your parents always? When does it become difficult to keep God's commandment? Do you think parents should have a commandment on how to treat their children?

_____

_____

_____

_____.

Chapter 7

James 1:8

"Such a person is double-minded and unstable in all they do."

'**H**ere we go' thought Principal Allen as he walked into the PTA meeting. There had been a storm brewing between the basketball and debate teams. Practices were being missed as the season went on. Clearly the coaches and parents weren't happy. Ironically, all three teams: debate, boys' basketball, and girls' basketball were doing great; all were ranked in the top five in the state. He wondered if anybody was going to ask about education or the school's fundraising for the anniversary celebrations. On second thought he knew what the meeting was going to about: basketball and debate, nothing more or nothing less. He was prepared for this and had asked some of the student-athletes to come speak during the meeting so that the parents could experience their point of view.

"Good evening everybody. Thank you for coming to the meeting today, where we can discuss current issues going on in Galilee High. I'll open with prayer before introducing Principal Allen. Will you bow your heads and close your eyes. Heavenly Father thank you for this day. We don't deserve any of the blessings you have bestowed upon us, yet we still see you in every part of our lives. Thank you for your grace and mercy. We ask that you guide our minds and hearts in all matters concerning your glory and in your son's Jesus name we pray...amen. Thank you for your patience. Now we can get started, come on up Principal Allen" Coach Slater opened up the meeting.

"Hello all. Like Coach Slater said thanks for coming. We have some special guests tonight that will come update parents on the extracurricular activities that we have going on this year. Our first guest is our senior captain, Jabari Stills from our boys' basketball team. Please give him your attention while he updates us on their season" Principal Allen said as he walked away from the podium.

"Hey parents, how are you doing tonight?" Jabari started, "Well I'll be quick, our season is going great! We are currently undefeated and ranked third in the state's high school rankings. We are on pace to break the school record for wins and bring home the first state championship since Coach Slater was a player. Thank you for your time tonight."

"Thank you Jabari that was very informative and the parents should understand where the season is going. Next we will have up our other senior captain, Ms. Esther Love, from our girls' basketball team." Principal Allen again stepped down as he introduced her.

"Hello everybody," Esther shyly began, "Umm...we are having a really good season. We have a great group of girls and have yet to lose this year. We are ranked number one in the state which is really amazing. Like really amazing! Umm...yeah that's all."

"Thanks Esther for that update, can we give our girl's team a round of applause?" Principal Allen paused during the applause, "Okay lastly we will have Lionell Best come up to talk about our debate team"

"Hey parents what's good? Well your debate team is good that's what!" Lionell laughed at his own joke before continuing, "We have continued on the same note we left off on last year by winning all but one tournament this year. We are currently ranked number two in the state and we will try to bring home back-to-back championships.

"Thanks for all the students that came today to speak during tonight's PTA meeting. Now I will open up the floor to concerned parents" Principal Allen finished looking towards the crowd.

"Well Principal Allen I'll start by following up Lionell's comments on the debate team. You know why our debate team has one loss this year? Well I'll answer that question for you. We lost because the basketball team traveled for a game and didn't return home until three in the morning! The debate team had to wake up at 6 for their tournament and their two best debaters play basketball and were exhausted. Therefore they were forced to use stand-ins and lost a close debate to a team that their best players would have easily beaten. That's just wrong and this is just one tournament. Most of the time the kids miss debate practice and are forced to miss lunch, just to meet with Mrs. Slater. Something has to be done to equalize the importance of these activities" Mrs. Best passionately articulated.

Lionell just ducked his head. Although he was picked to talk about debate he just did it to keep his mom happy. He loved basketball like nothing else. It was the one thing his dad would talk to him about. Usually whatever else he and his dad talked about his mom constantly corrected his dad, until his dad just gave up talking. The fact that his mom was so hyped up about debate was embarrassing. Most of his teammates thought that he cared more about debate and that he was just playing basketball to fit in. This caused them to mess with him, because they figured he didn't care about basketball. All he wanted was to prove himself to his friends and make his dad proud while avoiding the wrath of his mom. Seemed like an easy task until he actually tried it.

"Why create equality if there is not equal power between the two? The basketball teams have the opportunity to help earn the school money by hosting games and winning state games. They also can send much more people to college; my son wouldn't have the money for school, but this team and their success is causing college coaches to offer him full rides to their institutions. I know that debate is academic and more prestigious to you smart folk, but basketball speaks volumes in a community that is just trying to get by" Mrs. Abdul-Rahim responded.

"Ladies, I understand both of your points of view. I think that it will be hard to level the playing field for the sport of basketball and debate. One of the reasons being that basketball has more student participants and also participate in games more often playing twice, even three nights a week. Debate often meets a couple weekends a month until the end of the season will ramp up. The time consumption is just different" Principal Allen intervened.

"Exactly what I was sayin!" exclaimed Mrs. Abdul-Rahim.

"Well, we need to find a common ground because this debate team does mean something to the students on it. And it is unfair to them that they have to choose one or the other most of the times" Mrs. Slater spoke up.

"We can move the guys' practices to the morning, since most of your debaters are male. That way you can have the afternoon for practice. That won't be an issue I don't think" Coach Slater added.

"What? No! Coach we do individuals before school. How are we supposed to get better if we have practice?" Malcolm spoke up for the first time this meeting. He truly loved the mornings and the individual skill work he was able to put in with his teammate Jabari and Mr. Stills. It was like a safe haven and a place where he could just lose himself in something that meant so much to him. He never took basketball seriously before his dad died, it was just something he was naturally good at. Now with his dad gone and nothing else for him to get his mind off being alone, basketball became his escape. Practice wasn't the same as the individual workouts because Mr. Stills wasn't there and Coach was dedicated to the team not just giving attention to Malcolm. The attention Mr. Stills showed Malcolm during these workouts meant so much to him he didn't know if he could give it up.

"Well, could debate practice in the morning?" Mrs. Abdul Rahim asked knowing how important those workouts were to her son.

"Umm. Yes we could try practicing in the morning. That is a fair compromise I suppose" Mrs. Slater replied.

"Thank you parents. I'm glad we could settle that. Next on the list tonight is the end of the year anniversary celebrations. We will be inviting people to come back to participate in events during homecoming weekend. We will need plenty of parent participation with things like a school barbecue, anniversary question and answering panel, and a homecoming carnival. Are there any volunteers or questions?" Principal Allen asked the PTA attendees.

"Umm I'm willing to help with the barbecue. I know my way around the grill and wouldn't mind helping with that event. I'd just have to make sure to get off work. So I'd need to know the dates and what would be required of me." Mr. Gaines responded from the back of the room.

"Well, you're our first volunteer Mr. Gaines, so I'll let you know as we get more information. If you want to send me your schedule, we could work around that in order to ensure no conflict. Are there any other volunteers?" Principal Allen smiled as he asked for more parent involvement.

"You said carnival right? Aren't these kids a little old for a carnival? What kind of carnival? I might be able to help with that, but I need to know what it is before I commit" Mrs. Reece responded.

"Those are great questions Mrs. Reece. I cannot answer all of them right now. We will have games and various stations that students will help to run. We are currently looking into getting big rides and some other attractions. We will need to find out how much it cost, but we want to do something that the community can enjoy" Principal Allen described.

"Okay well I guess I'll help. I can't promise nothin' but I'll do the best I can" Mrs. Reece concluded.

"Thanks so much Mrs. Reece! This meeting is running over time and I know that you all have busy lives so I'll let you off the hook and head home. I'll pray us out and as you leave we will have a sign up in the back of the room near the refreshments table" Principal Allen began, "Our father who art in heaven hallowed be thy name. Thy kingdom come thy will be down on Earth as it is in Heaven. Thank you God for this opportunity to meet and discuss your plans for this institution. I ask that we don't move without you leading us and that you bless your plans. I ask that you protect us until we meet again, keep us safe, and help us to grow closer to you. In Jesus name I pray, Amen. Goodnight everybody, have a great evening. Don't forget to sign up as you leave" Principal Allen closed the meeting.

Everybody stood up to leave. Most passed by the table without even thinking about signing up for the carnival. The only ones that ended up signing the sheet to help were the Slaters, who never passed up an opportunity to help the school. Principal Allen noticed the lack of participation and prayed that God would touch the hearts of the parents of Galilee High.

Chapter Review

1. Do you think that the focus in high school by parents should be on the academics of the school or the extracurricular activities?

   _____
   _____
   _____
   _____.

2. Is it okay for the Principal Allen not to push the academics of the school and discuss what the parents want to?

   _____
   _____
   _____
   _____.

3. Which side would you be on? Do you believe in the sheer number impact basketball has and its ability to include a great amount of people? Are you a fan of automatic college scholarships that debate can offer a smaller amount of students?

   _____
   _____

_____

_____.

4. Do you think the carnival will be a success? Do you think enough parents will participate?

_____

_____

_____

_____.

5. Do you think kids should specialize or be able to participate in as much as possible? Why?

_____

_____

_____

_____.

Chapter 8

Psalms 4:1

"Answer me when I call to you, O my righteousness God. Give me relief from my distress; be merciful to me and hear my prayer."

"**W**ell ladies, this is what we've been waiting for. A chance to prove to everybody that we have a team of girls that only know how to win. We have done it all year against tough opponents, bad referees, and hostile crowds. Tonight will be no different; we will be the most hated team out there with everyone cheering against us. But why would we want it any other way?!?! We have worked too hard to have it easy. It would have made all that work pointless and we worked this hard because we knew it would be tough and we needed to make sure we were tougher! Let's go prove to everyone that we are the best team in Kansas!!!" Coach finished his passionate pre-game speech, "Esther, madam captain, will you pray us in to the game tonight?"

"Of course Coach. Bow your heads ladies. Heavenly Father, thank you for another day. We ask that you watch over us tonight during this game. We ask that no one is injured and you keep us as we give out this work. Amen." Esther paused, "Aight everybody bring it in. We are going to win this game! Put your hand in here girls, all season long it's been us against the world, but you all know that if God is with us THEN..."

"WHO CAN BE AGAINST US!!?!!?"All the girls shouted as they broke the huddle and headed out the locker room for their state championship game.

The girls were ready to do battle for the final time this season, where they would try to finish up their undefeated season. They would be the first girls' team in Galilee High history to go undefeated. This victory would just be the latest entry in the history books for this team. They already held the record for most three pointers in a season, most wins, most steals, most points, and most dunks. As far as individual records go, Jamaica and Esther took turns rewriting the record books. Jamaica started off the season by breaking the record for most points in a game, by scoring 53 in the second game of the season. Esther then broke the record for most three pointers in a game, by hitting ten threes in one game in the middle of the year. The tandem became the first players to both score 40 points in the same game during the state tournament, which they used to get out of the first round. This team was by far one of the most exciting teams to watch in the country. Coach had a feeling that if they won state, they'd be invited to the National Championship Tournament in Florida. But first things first, they had to win state. The team they were facing was tough and the defending state champions.

Coach looked at his daughter and winked at her as he whispered to her, "Let's hoop!"

Jamaica smiled as she headed onto the court. She was excited for this game because there were tons of scouts in the crowd and it was a chance for her mentor and best friend Esther to finish the season with a win. She had bet Lionell that she would have a dunk this game, so she had to get one early. She wouldn't dare attempt one during crunch time. She flexed her calves, did a couple hops in place to warm up her legs, as she walked around shaking hands with the opponent before the tip. She looked up into the crowd and realized there was much more opposing fans than Galilee fans here today; must be the three hour drive that was keeping them from showing up in droves. She found her mom and family and waved to them smiling. She walked by Esther and they did their special fancy handshake that finished with them having one knee in the air in a karate pose. She asked her, "You ready?"

Esther replied, "Girl I was born for this!"

The referee threw the ball up for the tip-off and Jamaica easily won it, tipping it to Esther before breaking towards the rim. Esther threw it ahead without even taking a dribble and Jamaica caught it on the run taking off for a dunk! Jamaica pointed to Esther acknowledging the great pass. Coach jumped out of his seat clapping for the great start. Galilee back on defense now, Esther gambled on a pass and Jamaica slid over in help blocking the shot. She grabbed the rebound and passed it to Ashley, who threw it ahead to Esther for another easy two. Galilee High was up 4-0 already only 30 seconds into the game.

Galilee used their fast-paced tempo early to wear down the transition defense of the other team. By the end of the second they were leading by 8 points with control of the ball during the last possession. Esther sized her defender up, showed the right hand in-n-out to see if the girl guarding her was going to bite. She did. She nodded to Jamaica, before going right hand in-n-out hard before crossing back to her left hand as her defender fell and the crowd yelled in excitement. 6 seconds on the clock as Esther moved towards the rim, drawing Jamaica's defender before lofting it high towards the rim as Jamaica grabbed it finishing soft off the glass, as time expired giving Galilee a ten point lead heading into halftime.

"Whew! Esther you might have just ruined that girls life!!!!!" Jamaica yelled heading into the locker room for halftime.

"Hey what can I say? My handle dumb nice, these little girls ain't ready!" Jamaica laughed, "I'm just glad we ended up bringing that lead back to ten before the break. We need to keep them at bay and not give them any confidence."

"I couldn't have said that any better madam captain" Coach started, "Girls we played a great first half, executing the game plan nearly perfectly. We rebounded great and pushed the ball creating the tempo we wanted. I want us to remember that these girls that we are playing against are a good team and we don't want to give them anything easy. In this second half I want to remind you that they are a good shooting team and once hot they're tough to stop. So let's keep them from ever getting a good look at the basket and we will be the Kansas State champs at the end of the next sixteen minutes!"

As they headed out the locker room to warm up for the second half, Coach looked at the scoreboard. Galilee was up ten, leading 44-34, with his two stars leading the way. Esther, the senior leader, had fifteen points while Jamaica, the freshman phenom, followed with an additional fifteen points giving them thirty of the teams forty-four points. He knew that he needed to win this game with Esther graduating along with his best role players. This might be their last chance to win state for a while until his daughter's class matured. He was trying to convey a sense of urgency to the team without making them feel more pressure. It was a touchy situation. The thing that made it easier was Esther, he had never coached someone so determined and passionate. She made everybody on the team better while still getting buckets. Definitely the best guard in the country in his opinion and certainly the player of the year in the state. He was going to miss her after this season, but he reminded himself to enjoy these next sixteen minutes and just let her work.

The third quarter started just how Coach feared it might, with Galilee giving up three consecutive threes. This onslaught from downtown closed the gap to one before he was forced to call a timeout.

"Girls, we have got to close out on the shooters! We just talked about this exact situation and there's no reason that we should be surprised when they make open shots, they made it to State too!!! Let's get it together!" Coach yelled trying to motivate his girls.

"Hey Jamaica, take over time" Esther said as they walked back onto the floor. Jamaica simply responded with a head nod.

Esther received the ball out of bounds and called, "One, set up, set up" as she crossed half court. She attacked hard right, stopped on a dime as her defender kept moving and rose and hit a three pointer, increasing their lead to four. As the ball went out of bounds she began guarding the point guard full court. The guard cut to receive the ball, got it, and turned around as Esther was in the perfect position to pick the ball out of her hands. Esther then turned to find a streaking Jamaica for a two hand dunk. The opponent took the ball out again, with Esther again pressuring the point guard. The girl cut to get open and just as the ball was being passed in tripped over her own feet. Esther caught the pass and took one dribble laying up while getting fouled by the girl who had thrown the ball away. She screamed while flexing after finishing the and-one layup. She walked to the free throw line, calmly knocking down the easy one. The opposing team's coach called a timeout quickly, angrily yelling while her team walked off the floor. Quickly their one point lead had become 9 with less than one minute coming off the clock, as Esther reminded all in the gym why she was considered one of the best players in all the land.

"Yes!" Coach yelled as the girls ran towards him on the sideline, "That's how we play Lioness basketball!!"

Galilee rode the momentum Esther created through the rest of the third quarter and finished with their ten point lead in tact. With three minutes left in the game Esther picked up her fourth foul, reaching in the backcourt, causing Coach Slater to sit her down to keep her from fouling out the game. Esther pointed at Jamaica as she walked off the floor, letting her know it was her time. They were only up five as their leader walked off the floor. It looked like a switch was flipped on Jamaica's face as she began grimacing with intensity, looking like her favorite player, Kobe Bryant.

First play out the timeout their opponents ran an out of bounds play where their player caught it heading towards the rim. It looked like an easy layup, before Jamaica came from the backside to block the shot off the backboard, causing all the Galilee fans to stand up cheering. She collected the rebound and sprinted up court, stopping on a dime at three point line where she hesitated, causing her defender to leave her feet and give Jamaica a free lane. She moved swiftly passed her first defender, before meeting the center with a fake and a spin move back to her left hand finishing off the glass. The crowd never had a chance to sit down as they continued to cheer their team on.

The other team brought the ball down court and the point guard tried to make a cross court pass on a flare screen, but Jamaica read it and picked it off with nobody in front. Someone from the crowd yelled, 'Bangout!' and she couldn't help taking off for another monstrous slam, her third of the game. A couple possessions later, after a couple turnovers by each team, Galilee High brought the ball up and the backup point guard Shyla passed it to Jamaica at the elbow. She faced up with a reverse pivot, head faked her defender, and jabbed her right, before taking a hard dribble left and stepping back behind the three point line leaving her defender frozen as she rose and sank a three pointer. Instantly she put up her three goggles and pointed right at Esther, who was up off the bench waving a towel and cheering loudly for her teammates.

Jamaica sensing a breaking point in their opponent, pretended to run down the floor, before quickly turning and stealing the inbounds pass and calmly stepping behind the three point line knocking down back-to-back threes putting the dagger into their opponents. Galilee took a fifteen point lead with two minutes to go in the game. Coach sent Esther back into the game, purely for theatrics. As the game closed out, he subbed out his starters one by one, leaving Esther for last coming off the floor with one minute remaining. Esther finished up her senior year with a thirty-five point game and state title, something she had been dreaming about for the past four years. She cried as she walked off to a standing ovation, hugging her coach thinking about all the tough times they had overcome together on this long journey of fighting for not only wins, but the program in general together.

Coach told Esther, "I'm so proud of you, you are one of the best players and people I've ever been around in my life. This was an amazing journey thank you for taking it with me. You are the Galilee High girls' program! Thanks for putting us on the map."

Esther responded simply through tears, "I love you coach. Thanks for everything!"

The crowd stood and cheered their team on as the game came to a close and the Galilee High Lionesses were crowned the Girls State Champions in Kansas!!!

Chapter Review

1. Have you ever performed under a lot of pressure? How was the performance? Did you do better or worse due to the pressure?

   _____
   _____
   _____
   _____.

2. Do you think that a state championship can help a school improve? Why or why not?

   _____
   _____
   _____
   _____.

3. Do you think the community should support a sports team trying to win a state championship even if they aren't a part of the school?

   _____
   _____
   _____
   _____.

4. Have you ever been nervous and someone else's confidence rubbed off on you? What happened?

_____
_____
_____
_____.

5. When you are in trouble do you call on God for help and protection? Is that the only time you call on God's name?

_____
_____
_____
_____.

Chapter 9

Psalms 144:1

Praise be to the Lord my Rock, who trains my hands for war, my fingers for battle.

'I can't believe we won it all' Coach thought to himself as he hit the road heading to the boys' state game. The fact that his teams had a chance to run the table in Kansas was amazing. The only thing that made him regret this success was this long late night drive he had to make to the game. He was leaving Topeka where the girls were and heading to Wichita. It was a tad bit over two hours on one of the most boring highways in America. He yawned as his eyes closed for a split second. Man he was drained from celebrating with his team. He was getting sleepy, he needed a conversation.

He called his wife, no answer. 'Dang' he thought, 'she must be sleep already.' He rubbed his eyes and turned up the radio to no avail because there weren't any stations out this way. His head drooped and his eyes closed for about ten seconds, he awoke to a loud horn blast from a semi-truck because he had swerved into the wrong traffic lane. He screamed and overcorrected, careening into the ditch on the opposite side of the highway flipping the car over three times before eventually landing upside down.

Jabari woke up and threw his pillow at Lionell. "Yo lil bro wake up! We are going to get some shots up man we have a state championship to win" Jabari yelled across the room.

"Come on man, it's 6 in the morning can't we go at 7?" Lionell groaned.

"Naw man we gotta be back for breakfast at 9. We need time to shoot and come back and shower. And you know how long you take in the bathroom Liona" Jabari laughed as he got out the bed.

"Aight man let's go. I'll call Malcolm you know he'll want to go." Lionell rolled out the bed and grabbed his phone, "Yo Malcolm wake up meet us at the gym we about to put in this work for tonight."

"Hey man what he say?" Jabari asked.

"He'll be there man, you know he don't miss workouts" Lionell responded.

Malcolm got up and went to the bathroom to brush his teeth. He thought about waking up Keith his roommate, but he remembered last time he tried that and Keith swung on him. He finished up and walked out the room meeting Jabari and Lionell downstairs. They headed out of the hotel and across the street to the gym with all three carrying a basketball. They began working out; starting with ball handling and moving towards jumpers.

"Hey you know they're going to play zone, we will have to make jumpers tonight to win" Jabari told his teammates.

"Speak for yourself. All zone means for me is body count! I'm going to catch at least three people slipping tonight. Easy!" Lionell guaranteed as he shot his jumper.

"Yeah you're the jump shooter Jabari I'm going to be slashing them gaps all day long and they better not dare play man to man. Because they will get cooked and I'll eat them alive!" Malcolm said making another one of his jumpers.

"Hey Jabari your phone ringing!" Lionell alerted him.

"Thanks man I ain't even hear it" Jabari said running to his bag, "Hello, huh? Hold up Pops what you talking about? Slow down, what happened to Coach? He's in the hospital? What happened? Aight we on our way! Hey fellas we have to go back to the hotel Coach had an accident on his way here from the girl's state win" Jabari said running to grab his ball and bag.

"What did you just say? Hey man wait up!" Lionell yelled following Jabari out of the gym.

"I know he didn't say Coach got in an accident! That just can't be true man!" Malcolm stuttered as he walked out of the gym.

Mrs. Slater cried as she headed to a hospital in the middle of nowhere. Jamaica just sat in the passenger seat shocked and confused. Her dad was a big strong man who never got hurt. Even in the NBA playing against those giants he never was injured and he always answered her call. Now they were headed somewhere, in the middle of nowhere where they were claiming her dad was in critical condition.

Mr. Jacobi Stills called all the parents rooms and let them know that Coach had been in an accident and wasn't going to make it to the game tonight. He wanted to know if they thought they should play tonight or forfeit the game. They needed to have a meeting about what was going to happen next.

Mrs. Kierra Reece hit her line of cocaine after hearing the news; she had been trying to quit, but it seemed like bad news always forced her back to her habit. She couldn't stomach what losing coach would do to the psyche of her son, Keith. The cocaine gave her stability, it was always there for her when she needed it. "Hello" she answered her phone, "Yeah baby I heard, I'm heading up there today." She hung up and grabbed her keys wiping her nose as she walked out of the door.

Mrs. Louise Best called her son and told him she was on the way. She shook her head thinking about the tragedy that was taking place. Her first thought was that if Lionell never played basketball, then he wouldn't be experiencing the heartbreak of someone close to you being near death. 'That's no way to think' she told herself as she called her husband and told him the news. She was going to go pick him up on her way out of the city.

Mr. Trayvon Gaines was over at the twins' apartment building when he heard the news about Coach. He called over the building supervisor, "Hey, how have the boys been?"

"They've been great. No noise complaints or anything like that" the supervisor said.

"How about Carter? That's the taller one. Has he been keeping late nights? Women around their apartment?" Mr. Gaines asked.

"I really shouldn't be telling you this," the supervisor paused, "but he keeps late nights oftentimes meets people in the lobby and takes them up to the room. Not many women mostly young men. I don't think he's selling drugs, but he's making money somehow."

"Hmm. Interesting thank you sir. I'll try to see what he has going on. Well here's the money for the next couple months go ahead and give me the rent they've paid." Mr. Gaines said as he took the money from the supervisor.

"If you don't mind me asking what do you do with their money sir?" Supervisor asked walking Mr. Gaines out of the building.

"I take it and invest it so they can buy a car or start their own business when they go to college. They'll get scholarships so school will be paid for, but this money will be of some use to them once they get down there." Mr. Gaines said leaving the apartment.

The team gathered in the hotel banquet hall; Mr. Jacobi Stills had asked management to let them use it. The players, some still waking up unaware of the purpose of this meeting, were chatting and looking for Coach.

"I know some of you know why we're having this meeting, but to those who don't, Coach was injured in a bad car accident on his way here after the girl's game.

His car flipped multiple times and he is in critical condition right now at the hospital. You know we don't have an assistant coach, so I called this meeting to see if you guys still wanted to play tonight and who would you want to coach the team tonight?" Mr. Stills finished.

"Well let's vote. I think Coach would want us to finish what we started and win tonight instead of quitting" Jabari spoke up.

"Yeah, let's vote" Keith agreed, "All those in favor of playing raise your hand." Every single player raised their hands.

Mr. Stills smiled, because he knew what their response would be before he asked. He knew how resilient these kids were. "Well who should coach?" Mr. Stills asked.

"Why don't you coach us?" Malcolm asked, "You come to most of the practices you're at all the games. I speak for most everybody when I say we trust your judgement."

"I would be honored to sit on the bench with you guys tonight. We won't have a pregame shoot around today with the team. If you want to go shoot you can between noon and two when we have the gym. We will eat our pregame meal at 4:30 just meet here in the lobby." Mr. Stills told the team, just repeating what he and Coach had discussed the day before.

People filed into the arena for the Kansas state championship game, while the players sat in the locker room getting ready. News had come from the hospital that Coach was stable, but not conscious yet. He had suffered very severe injuries, but they were able to stabilize his breathing and internal bleeding. This caused somewhat of relief with the players and they were praying that his condition continued to improve.

"Hey y'all check this out" Martin spoke up, "we have an opportunity to do what God has prepared for us. Some people are meant to paint, others meant to build, some are meant to explore. God has prepared us under the tutelage of one of his servants to play basketball. We have been taught the right way to play and how our play glorifies God's name. Now I can't honestly say that God is concerned with wins and losses of high school basketball games, but I do know that whatever we do we do in the name of God and I pray that we go to battle today and do what the Lord has prepared us to do."

"Yeah what my ugly brother said. Let's go get buckets, we worked too hard to not bring this game back to the city" Carter added.

The team came out of the tunnel in their black and gold jerseys to a standing ovation. It seemed like the entire community had come out to support the team.

The team they were playing against had their fair share of fans and the stands were packed for tonight's affair.

"Welcome ladies and gentleman, men, women, and children to this year's boys' state championship game! We will have Galilee High versus West Kansas Academy, two great teams who have had great seasons. Galilee High appears tonight without their coach, Coach Slater, who was in a bad accident on the way here. Can we please have a moment of silence in honor of his absence and pray for his recovery?" The announcer paused briefly before continuing. "Thank you. Let's introduce to the starting lineups for tonight. First the visiting team, West Kansas Academy, who will start 6' point guard James Peterson, 6'4" shooting guard who's heading to the University of Kansas next year Greg Byers, 6'3" forward Hugh Watson, 6'4" forward Mason Banks, and their big guy in the middle also heading to the University of Kansas 7'0" Curtis Staley. Give it up for the West Kansas Academy starting 5! Now over to the home team Galilee High! Their starting five includes: senior leader and captain 6'2" point guard Jabari Stills, their big guy in the middle officially signed to University of Missouri Kansas City 6'9" Keith Reece, 6'6" Martin Gaines at forward, 6'5" Lionell Best on the other wing, and 6'4" Malcolm Abdul-Rahim at the other guard position. Give a huge round of applause for your Galilee High Lions!" The announcer finished his introductions.

"Hey fellas bring it in. This is something that we've prayed for and now God has answered our prayers, giving us an opportunity to leave everything we have on this basketball court, on the biggest stage so far in your young lives." Mr. Stills began his pre-game speech, "Now this game is going to come down to you seniors, all year long Coach has given the games to you guys and allowed you to win them. Tonight will be no different. This is Coach's fourth year here at Galilee and in honor of that only the guys who have bled and sweat each step of the way will play tonight. That means you Jabari, Keith, Lionell, Martin, and Carter will have to win this game for us tonight. I believe in you and I know you believe in yourselves so let's get this win and bring this trophy back home for Coach!"

Galilee High came out jittery in the first quarter and by the middle of the quarter was down 9 points, thanks to West Kansas Academy's star guard scoring 13 of their 17 points.

"Hey Carter it's your time son. Flame on!" Mr. Stills yelled down his bench. "Hey I need you to stop Byers, he's killing us man!"

"Oh that should be fun. I love locking up guys who think they can go. It would be my honor to get us back in this game" Carter let his coach know as he ran to the scorer's table to check in.

They didn't call Carter the 'human torch' for nothing. As soon as he stepped on the court, he hit a corner three pointer off of a drive and kick by Jabari. Then came down and stole a pass intended for Byers and threw down a thunderous windmill that ignited the crowd like wildfire. The fast break dunk also cut the lead to 4 in just thirty seconds. West Kansas Academy threw the ball down low, where Keith was tiring from battling with their 7 ft. center, and he made a tough drop step hook over Keith's outstretched hands that made their lead 6 with twenty seconds to go. Carter called for the ball on the wing screaming, "I'm hot! Send that my way!" Malcolm got him the rock with ten seconds left. Carter pump faked, jabbed right, took one hard dribble left, before stepping back and shooting over Byers outstretched hands. Before the ball went through the goal, Carter turned around and put both hands in the air signaling the shot was good. The crowd erupted as the ball swished through the net ending the first quarter with Galilee High down three after one.

The second quarter was filled with back and forth action, with each senior taking a turn to keep Galilee in the game. At the beginning of the quarter, big Keith got his revenge on Staley, making a beautiful up and under move, drawing the foul and getting the bucket. He came down the next possession and caught Staley helping uphill catching a lob from Lionell and dunking on the seven footer drawing another and-one and sending

Staley to the bench with his third foul. After Keith got the crowd going, Lionell kept them into it with a couple of his high flying attacks on the rim. One ending in a full up and under that he just got off heading to the ground. The next foray to the rim was finished off by a two hand thunderous dunk that left the goal shaking long after he came down, giving Galilee their first lead of the game at 35-34 with four minutes left in the second. After that Malcolm and Martin took over, stretching the Galilee lead to ten, each scoring five on jumpers. Malcolm's coming off of Martin's screens and Martin's coming off of Malcolm's passes. They maintained this lead going into halftime with Carter playing a huge role, as he held Byers to only two free throws during that stretch. The only problem was Galilee only playing six at this pace was tiring towards the end of the quarter and gave up a couple easy buckets giving West Kansas Academy life heading into the half only down six, after the Galilee spirited onslaught.

Mr. Stills walked into the hallway during halftime took a deep breath. That half had many ups and downs, but ultimately they had come away with a lead. His only questions were would West Kansas Academy's two best players turn up to a different level? Their big guy was in foul trouble in the second and that played a role in some of Galilee's wings having driving lanes to the rim. He also knew that they used a ton of their energy up in that first half playing with the spirit of winning for their injured coach. He wondered if that energy would last them the entire game. He walked into the locker room and looked around at the young men sitting in there and smiled because these might be the greatest group of young men he'd ever been around.

"Hey guys I know we're tired, but that's not a reason to quit. I remember what Coach told me one day when we were discussing Christianity. He told me, 'Grace is the reason we are saved, because when we are tempted we often fail. That's not a reason to quit though, just because we are tired is a weak reason to stop walking like Christ. If God brings us to something you can be sure that he will bring us through it.' That relates tonight as I look at this group of guys that I love and that have pushed me to find life this year, when I thought it was impossible. After my dad died I had no direction. Coach gave me that, but he also showed me who Christ is. Win or lose we leave everything we have on that basketball floor. Because that is what Christ has allowed us to do. So let's play basketball!" Malcolm yelled as he ran out of the locker room leading the Lions onto the floor for the second half.

This pep talk seemed to work for a moment as the Lions began taking over early in the third quarter. A rare Lionell three and a put back layup by Keith put the Lions up eleven early. Then the University of Kansas signees took over the game making shot after shot. Big Staley's physical presence began to wear on Keith and they fed him relentlessly until Mr. Stills had to give Keith a break and call a timeout. By the time the time-out was taken, Galilee was down 5 points with three minutes left in the third quarter. After the timeout, it was Byers turn to takeover. He hit three tough threes over Martin's outstretched hands; on one of them Martin even poked him in the eye. After the third one Byers swept the ground with three fingers on each hand causing their crowd to go crazy! Mr. Stills called another timeout trying to stop the bleeding with the Lions down 14 after the three consecutive threes by Byers.

Jabari came to the bench upset, punching the chair in disgust. "Hey pops let's go zone and every time that big guy touches it, I'm taking it! Have Carter shade Byers and he'll take him out of the game and we will win."

Mr. Stills looked at the rest of the team and asked them, "Well, what do y'all think?"

"He's a captain for a reason sir. He sees stuff we don't. Let's do it. Put Carter in for me, I'm tired man" Keith spoke up.

"Okay let's do it then. Bring it in FAMILY ON THREE. ONE, TWO, THREE!" Mr. Stills screamed.

"FAMILY" the team yelled.

The rest of the game was something that the Lions had seen all season; their captain dominating both ends of the floor. Jabari just took over and every single time Staley touched the ball Jabari was there reaching and harassing him. He forced Staley to turn the ball over five consecutive times, with the fifth time resulting in Staley getting a technical foul for complaining about the lack of a call. His coach had to pull him out the game just to calm him down. At this point Jabari began doing what he did best: relentlessly attacking the rim every single possession. It started with a right hand floater in the lane. This move was followed by a spin move up and under finish that got 'oohs' and 'ahhs' from the crowd. This continued throughout the rest of the third quarter causing West Kansas Academy's coach to call all of his timeouts in an effort to stop him. After using his last timeout, he didn't even get up from the bench, just continued yelling at his guys to figure it out for themselves.

As the buzzer sounded ending the game, ending an effort by Galilee High that news stations would call awe inspiring; the crowd stormed the court and the players collapsed on the floor in sheer joy. They had done it! They had won the game! They had brought a state championship back to Galilee High; the first of its kind since Coach Slater himself was in a jersey. The boxscore showed how far the program had come since the beginning. It was a testament to the skill development talent of not only Coach Slater, but also the hard work that the players put in outside of the team as well. Jabari Stills, who once was touted in the city as the best guard who couldn't lead a team, ended the game with 25 points (twenty coming in the second half), 9 assists, and 5 steals. Lionell Best, the guy who was just happy to play, finished the game with 14 loud points; several coming on dunks at the rim. Big Keith Reece, the guy Coach had to beg to play, dominated down low finishing his career with 17 points and 20 rebounds. The twins: Carter and Martin were double trouble as usual, finishing with a combined 43 points and 10 steals, giving the crowd plenty to cheer for. Malcolm was the star of the show scoring a game high 35 points, just continually being in the right place at the right time and only missing three shots. He broke down in tears as he hugged his mom and she told him how proud she was and how proud his father would have been. This was a perfect ending to a season except one thing that was missing; coach was still in the hospital. The rest of the ceremony was bittersweet because when they received their medals and the state championship trophy, they were all thinking about their coach who was in the hospital fighting for his life.

Chapter Review

1. Do you think it is Mrs. Slater's fault Coach crashed? Have you ever blamed somebody for something? Do you think forgiveness is possible?

   _____

   _____

   _____

   _____.

2. Do you think they should have played the game knowing that Coach was fighting for his life?

   _____

   _____

   _____

   _____.

3. Do you think sport can bring people together or cause people to be distracted from 'more' important things?

   _____

   _____

   _____

   _____.

4. Have you ever been in Malcolm's position and done something hoping it would make a loved one that has passed on proud? How did you feel after you completed your goal?

_____
_____
_____
_____.

5. Do you believe that God has a plan for you and prepares you for success? Have you asked God to reveal his plan for your life?

_____
_____
_____
_____.

Chapter 10

1 Chronicles 4:10

"Jabez cried out to the God of Israel, "Oh, that you would bless me and enlarge my territory! Let your hand be with me, and keep me from harm so that I will be free from pain." And God granted his request."

*T*he Galilee High Debate team had finished off the season on a long winning streak. After losing a couple of early tournaments due to exhaustion from the late night basketball games, to the early morning turnarounds. The team figured it out from there on out and dominated the rest of Kansas debate season. Lionell won Debater of the Year and he and Carter were invited to the National Debate Tournament. Mrs. Slater was Coach of the Year for a second consecutive year. The National Debate Tournament was in Hollywood,

California, so the kids were excited to get a trip there to see the movie stars. They would have to fly and thanks to some fundraisers during the year they were able to fly for free.

"Hey now, I know we are going to Hollywood, but we aren't going to see movie stars. We are going to bring home a National Title. Something that has never happened before at Galilee High. Let's become a part of history this week" Mrs. Slater reminded the team of their mission as they boarded the plane to California.

"Man I can't wait to get there!" Carter screamed, "I got a fresh cut and I know I can get at least three B-List celebrity girls and one model to holla at ya boy."

"Boy stop! High school girls barely want to talk to you. Nobody in their right mind in Hollywood will have a conversation with you, let alone give you their numbers!" Jamaica laughed.

"Yeah looking at the schedule we will be hard-pressed to find some free time anyways. Carter, they have us busy doing a lot of things outside of the actual tournament. A lot of sight-seeing and historical landmarks we will get to go see. Seems pretty cool actually!" Gerell inserted.

"Yeah that's what I'm excited about, we will win the tournament easy! I'm there to learn about the history of Hollywood!" Howard agreed.

"Man y'all lame, it won't be any stars at the tourist spots. We have to figure out where locals go, and hit those spots. There's some girls on Disney Channel that my mom wouldn't mind me bringing home!" Carter told everybody as he took his seat on the plane.

"Lord help us all!" Exclaimed Jamaica as she took her seat next to her mom.

The flight was uneventful, as most of the kids slept and the plane didn't hit many rough spots. Once in Hollywood, they had a day to rest and sight see before the tournament started. Mrs. Slater decided they would just rest because she wanted them focused for the tournament. She knew the difference in state competition and national competition and she wanted them to be ready for that upgrade.

"Man ya moms mad wack for making us stay in the hotel today! We could be out seeing the world, instead we gotta stay in this wack hotel" Lionell told Jamaica as they walked to the pool.

"At least they have a pool. A little sunshine and water ain't never been a bad idea. I could get use to this California weather no doubt!" Jamaica responded.

"Yeah this weather is nice. Speaking of California I just received an offer from Stanford. It is academic though, I really think I can play basketball on the next level. I may pursue something like that instead" Lionell said as they sat down next to the pool.

"Stanford is a great school Li, maybe you should see if you can walk on there? That might be the best opportunity for you" Jamaica said.

"Don't call me Li in public, man that's embarrassing! And the only thing about walking on is that they might not give me playing time. I don't want to work so hard for a team that I don't get to contribute to. You know?" Lionell asked her thoughts.

Yeah, I understand, but it is in California. That has to count for something right?" Jamaica reminded him.

"I suppose. I mean I'm more concerned with the school than I am its location. It would be nice, but if I can find a good academic school that wants me as a basketball player too, then I'll go there instead. I know for someone like you with plenty of options location is important, but for me I just need to take the best opportunity. I don't have all those options. I don't get to shoot all game like you" Lionell mused.

"Stop all that! You know you can play and if your mom let you play AAU you'd have tons of offers on the table. Even on the Galilee film, dad often talked about how athletic you were and how colleges would be drooling over you if they knew who you were. So stop selling yourself short Li!" Jamaica said blushing as she said the nickname she gave him.

"Sorry to get off topic, but I miss ya pops. Is he doing any better?" Lionell asked somberly.

"I mean not really. He hasn't regained consciousness or anything. It's so crazy to see him laid up in that bed looking so broken. I mean all my life my dad has been so strong and always there for me. Now my mom tells me I have to be there for him and keep praying, but I don't know how to be as strong as I need to be" Jamaica said as she teared up.

"Sorry for bringing it up. Didn't mean to make you sad. It's just like everything is different without him. Like school is quiet. The gym has lost its pull, I haven't shot a basketball in weeks! He was definitely a second father to me, but it's like I didn't realize it until he wasn't there anymore" Lionell said holding Jamaica as she cried.

"Yeah," she sputtered through sobs, "My dad was everywhere I needed him. At home, school, gym...everywhere I didn't want him to be he was there too. Like this trip is so bittersweet. I can't believe my mom would leave him right now in his weakest moment. She told me that he would want us to go and represent Galilee High. That if we win we would make him proud. Can you at least make sure that happens Lionell? This is just as much for Coach as winning state was. I need this for my emotional stability. If we come all this way and lose while my hero, my father, is fighting for his life, then it might break the little mental health I have left."

"I understand shawty, I'll do all I can and the rest is in God's hands. Heavenly Father, I know that you see us hurting God. We don't know your plans nor do we know how this situation is supposed to go according to your will, but we do know when your children cry out you listen. Father, we are crying out for your love to cover us and comfort us in this time. We ask that you heal Coach Slater and that he makes a full recovery and can testify to the fact that you are good and just. We know that he is one of your soldiers and we need him in this battlefield. We are searching for answers God and we just ask that you provide peace of mind and spirit. Be with us while we are here and enlarge our territory Father as you did with your servant Jabez in the word. Amen" Lionell finished his prayer and they just laid by the pool watching others swim and enjoy life. It seemed so odd to them that nobody else in the hotel was going through something. It finally hit them that God was reminding them that joy is everlasting and not a fleeting emotion. This gave them the strength to get up and head back to their rooms satisfied with the peace God had provided them at the moment.

God showed favor to the Galilee High Debate team in Hollywood. They were put in a favorable bracket with mostly teams that were at nationals for the very first time. Also they never had to argue negative in any debate during the entire tournament. The last final debate of the tournament they were matched up with a team from Chicago, Illinois that had won three national titles in the past six years. Mrs. Slater was nervous because she had actually talked to the coach from the other team on several occasions to ask questions about how to build a successful debate team in the inner city. This team was very successful and had the most national championships of any debate team in the country! They also were inner city with 98% of their students being below the poverty line and receiving free or reduced lunch. This program shined brightly amongst the school's programs; being a member of the debate team almost always meant receiving a full college scholarship and a way out of their current circumstances. It was this program that Mrs. Slater had modeled the Galilee High program after and now it was up to her students to take down this high powered program.

"Lionell and Carter you've been amazing this tournament and I expect nothing less today. We again have the affirmative which puts us at a great advantage. Let's win this tournament so we can go back home with our heads held high!" Mrs. Slater encouraged her team.

"Hey Carter remember what I said man. We need this one" Lionell reminded his friend.

"Yeah, of course I got you man" Carter reassured him.

The judges were waiting as the Galilee High Lions entered the room. They were dressed to impressed, with Lionell wearing a black suit with gray stripes accented by his white shirt with a gold, black and gray tie that put the outfit together perfectly. Carter had the suit that Coach let him borrow earlier that year. He had a double-breasted all gray 'power suit' with gray and black Stacy Adams on that matched perfectly with his black dress shirt and the gray tie he wore as well. They were dressed like they were going to win the tournament and certainly felt that way as well.

"Mom don't they look mad cute? I'm glad a couple judges are women! We might low key get their votes just because our team looks better!" Jamaica joked.

"Yeah they are handsome young men. Remember you're too young to date though so advert your eyes young lady!" Mrs. Slater laughed.

"Man they aight! I'm just saying I've seen better, like every morning I look in the mirror you feel me?" Gerell asked Jamaica.

"Boy in your dreams!" Jamaica laughed.

The finals started with the announcer introducing both teams and acknowledging the fact that Galilee High was the Kansas State Champions and the Chicago team was the Illinois State Champions. They welcomed all the guest and finally began the long awaited debate of the year for the right to be called National Champions.

"Welcome to the National Debate Championship Finals." The announcer began, "tonight we will have master debaters from Kansas: Lionell Best and Carter Gaines facing off against Chicago's finest: Tyrell James and Fred Oakley. This match is very significant in debate history; it is the first time in our tournament that we've had two all African-American teams face-off in the debate finals. It is truly an honor to be in the presence of these amazing young men as they try to become etched in debate history. Let us begin with the first constructive speech from the affirmative team Galilee High."

"Good evening judges, my competitors, and people of the audience. Thank you for giving me your ear. Tonight the resolve is that the federal government should adopt a nationwide policy to decrease overcrowding in prisons and jails in the United States. This is a problem because the programs that are funding these prisons are taking money away from other programs that could help the people that are imprisoned. An example is the problem America is facing with drugs. We could respond like Portugal and treat people with drug problems, instead of imprisoning them. We could use money to open up facilities that will help people beat the drug habits that are hindering their lives.

Instead we take an approach that is out of control and obviously not working. Our jails are thoroughly overcrowded and it isn't because we are at a point in our history where our citizens are more criminal in nature. In fact, crime is down across the country yet, the amount of people under the scrutiny of the penal system is at an all-time high. This is no coincidence. The system in place is running efficiently and effectively placing hordes of young men of color in jail, the penitentiary, or on probation. This is the major cause of overcrowding in the system at every level. A change in the drug laws and enforcement of those laws would effectively end the overcrowding of prisons and jails.

We need to end this problem because we are taking capable young people, men especially, who could contribute to society and help us as a nation and forcing them to become a part of a subordinate societal class. This class has no political power and struggles to economically contribute due to the barriers put in place to force them into the cyclical nature of the judicial system. We must move the money from building prisons and use that money to rehabilitate people that need help. We, as a country, need to refocus our efforts and reverse the systematic imprisonment of more people than ever seen in this world" Carter opened up the finals with a passionate speech.

As soon as he finished, you could see the Chicago team drop their heads and sulk. It was as if his premise was the same exact thing that they wished they were able to say. As he sat down Lionell dapped Carter for putting them in a great position to win. The Chicago team responded the best they could, but it just wasn't enough being in the finals unless the affirmative team slipped up and left open a loophole, you were pretty much doomed to lose. Lionell followed Carter and closed the match forcing any doubt in the judges minds that Galilee High Debate was the National Champion to disappear.

Jamaica looked at her mom with tears in her eyes and said, "Guess dad would be proud."

Mrs. Slater, tears streaming down her face, responded, "You are right baby girl. He would be so proud. I can't wait to show him the pictures and trophy. He'll be so impressed!"

Carter, Lionell, Gerell, and Howard allowed the ladies to have their moment and stood off to the side nodding their heads towards each other. Their nods acknowledged the mutual respect they had gained from each other throughout the season and also the end of a great season.

"Hey man, real talk, I love y'all" Carter said to his teammates.

"Man I love y'all too! Real talk, I just ain't wanna be the first to say it. Thanks Carter for biting that bullet" Howard admitted.

"Yeah man this has been one of the greatest experiences of my life! I truly appreciate each and every one of you" Gerell showed love to his friends.

"Yeah man it's been real no lie. Back to Kansas City, seems like it came too fast" Lionell shook his head.

"Naw, man we got what we needed from Hollywood. Let's go change the lives of those who need us back home" Carter said nodding towards the Slater women, who were still crying.

"Yeah you're right gotta take care of the family" Lionell agreed.

Chapter Review

1. Do you think that Mrs. Slater and Jamaica should have left home for the tournament with Coach in the hospital?

   _____
   _____
   _____
   _____.

2. Would you leave some of your family in order to achieve something you thought would make them proud? Why or why not?

   _____
   _____
   _____
   _____.

3. Do you think that going to different places is important to developing as a person? Why or why not?

   _____
   _____
   _____
   _____.

4. Do you believe that americans have a drug problem? Why or why not? Do you know three people that use illegal drugs or abuse legal drugs?

_____

_____

_____

_____.

5. Have you ever prayed for a ton of things and God says yes to some of your prayer? How does that make you feel? Do you keep praying for the things that you haven't received an answer for?

_____

_____

_____

_____.

Chapter 11

Psalms 46:10

"Be still, and know that I am God. I will be exalted among the nations, I will be exalted in the earth!"

"Now we have the privilege to hear from one of our very own, Coach Josiah Slater! As most of you know he suffered a nearly life-ending car crash a couple months ago. He was in a coma for weeks and just recently began walking again. The fact that he is here and willing to share with us is a miracle. I can't wait to hear what he has to say. With no further ado here is the keynote speaker of this year's Galilee High closing banquet, Coach Josiah Slater!" Principal Allen finished to a standing ovation, prepared for the man everyone in the room admired.

"Thank you for the applause. It is all for God's glory that I'm here today. Let me open in prayer before beginning tonight if you don't mind. Heavenly Father, thanks for another day. Truly it is a blessing to be here and I can never take that for granted again. I ask that you silence me and my flesh and use the Holy Spirit to speak through me. Allow those in attendance to hear and be able to use what I say to grow closer to you. Amen.

Now let's get started tonight I have the privilege to bring the ending year message to the Galilee High family. I used to wonder how they pick people to do things like this. Well now I know, you have to go through some near death experience" Coach Slater paused as he laughed at his own joke before continuing, "Be careful what you wish for people. Well if you have your Bible turn to Psalms 46:10 that's where my message today will stem from. It reads, 'Be still, and know that I am God. I will be exalted among the nations, I will be exalted in the earth!' I love to pick apart scripture and delve into each section of every sentence that the Lord gives us.

So the first part is 'Be still.' Well what does that mean to us today? What does stillness truly look like? Well in my life stillness looked like: my car flipping multiple times, me losing control of my body, and slipping into a coma. God had to take me to the extreme of stillness to get me to a point that I listened to Him and realized that He is God. Now I hope God doesn't have to completely immobilize you in order for you to 'Be still.' In scripture we see that God uses various methods to get our attention. He had to tell Moses to 'Be Still' by communicating through a burning bush. He got Paul, renamed Saul, to be still by blinding him on the road to Damascus. What will it take for you to 'Be still' and listen to God?

The next part of the scripture is 'know that I am God.' Well what does that knowledge look like? Who is God? Well let's turn to Galatians 5:22-23 'But the fruit of the Spirit is love, joy, peace, patience, kindness, goodness, faithfulness, gentleness, and self-control. Against such things there is no such law.' These things highlight the personality traits of God and also shows us what traits we as believers are called to have. Let us also turn to 1 John 4:8 'Whoever does not love does not know God, because God is love.' So if we reverse that statement we can say that to know God is to love God. And one more scripture for this point, John 14:15 'If you love me, you will obey what I command.'

So much in this last part of the sentence 'know that I am God.' Because we see in scripture to know God, is to love God, and to love God is to obey what He commands. If you want to know what He commands you must pick up this book! This Holy Bible that He provides us with has advice for every situation; He shows us how to love, how to show grace, and how to walk in righteousness. You must read God's word to get to know Him. You must pray and meditate, in order to understand His love for us. That takes time which is why sometimes He forces us to 'Be still' because He knows how much of Him we need in order to fully walk in our purpose.

The last part of this verse I think is the hardest part for most Christians to understand. It reads 'I will be exalted among the nations, I will be exalted in the Earth.' This verse explicitly says that God will receive praise, and this praise is non-conditional. What I mean by that is that God will be exalted regardless of what we do, what we say, what we think. It takes complete humbleness for us as Christians to remind ourselves that our works are like filthy rags and God doesn't need them. He doesn't need us, it says 'I will be exalted' not I need you to exalt me.

We sometimes forget this fact, that God created us and like all creators you don't need your creation. Your creation serves a purpose yes, but you existed before your creation, not because of your creation. God created us for a function and that function is to bring glory to His name and honor His righteousness. That is why we are here! We were created in His image, both male and female in order to bring glory to the name of the Lord. This verse truly holds true to my heart because I got caught up in my works. I thought that the more I did for God the better I was, the more righteous I was. God had to remind me that He alone was good and I was here to give Him glory. I am a broken, dirty human being, but God has cleansed me and now through Him I will bring Him glory.

I know now my purpose is to glorify God in all I do and depend on him for everything that I do. No matter how strong we think we are, we are weak and limited in our abilities. We must 'Be still, and know that He is God. He will be exalted among the nations, He will be exalted in the earth!'

Thank you for listening to me tonight, it is truly humbling that you would honor me with your attention. I truly hope that through the Holy Spirit, the words that I've said tonight ring true and help you become closer to our Heavenly Father. If I could wrap up my speech tonight in prayer I'll be out of your hair. O God, we humble ourselves before you and thank you for reminding us that we need you. I ask that you still your people so that we are reminded through all this noise that you are Lord and your name is to be exalted among all the earth. Amen." Coach walked slowly back to his seat on the stage as everyone in attendance stood on their feet and applauded his sermon.

Principal Allen walked back to the podium, "Thanks Coach I think we definitely need to be reminded to be still and get to know God. Amen. That is what Galilee High is about; we promote relationship with Christ on an interpersonal level. This relationship helps to create leaders that can come back and edify their communities. Men like Coach Slater and women like his wife, Mrs. Slater, I mean Dr. Slater, congratulations on her finishing her doctorate degree by the way. Well, people like them are the reason that Galilee High exists and we hope to continue to create Christian leaders that are socially responsible and capable of impacting Wyandotte County. Thank you all for coming tonight you are welcome to visit our booths that highlight some of the things that we have accomplished this past year. We love you all and we thank you for supporting Galilee High, the place where the Lion's heart of Wyandotte County resides" Principal Allen finished his speech with his old lion's heart spill. The kids think it's corny, but they never forget it and that's the point. Galilee High is also a place very few people forget once becoming a part of the family. Galilee High is a place of love and truly shines a light into Wyandotte County, driving away darkness.

Chapter Review

1. Do you ever take time to reflect on God, His Word, and His plan that he has for you? Take the time now to just pray and ask God to reveal Himself in your life. Write down what God reveals to you here. Really listen, give it at least ten minutes of quiet reflection before writing.

_____

_____

_____

_____

_____

_____

_____

_____

_____

_____

_____

_____

_____

_____

_____

_____

_____.

About the Author

Justin Strickland was born and raised in Kansas City, KS. He loves this city and after getting his Bacherlor's Degree in Sport Management from Culver-Stockton College in 2014 he returned to Kansas City to train for a professional basketball career. While waiting for a contract he began to volunteer at his alma mater Sumner Academy of the Arts & Sciences. This book was birthed during that time as he fell in love again with this city and these people. After playing professional basketball in Mexico for one season his professional basketball career ended. He finished his Master's Degree in leadership in 2019 and is still very involved in Kansas City. He is currently a college basketball coach, mentor, podcaster, personal trainer, husband, son, brother, and friend. If you want to give any feedback on the book send an email to hopeink@gmail.com!

Follow on social media
Instagram - @hopeinkc
Twitter - @hopeinkc
Facebook - Justin Strickland

www.ingramcontent.com/pod-product-compliance
Lightning Source LLC
Chambersburg PA
CBHW072357030726
47505CB00014B/1879